"Spanning the last century with narrators aged 10 to 100, these stories reveal women struggling to fit a definition of womanhood that cannot contain them. By employing forms that break with convention in the same spirited ways her characters do, Laura Krughoff creates a world of stunning detail that examines just what people will do when expectations stifle truth. In *Wake in the Night*, we are reminded why we must push beyond easy categories and find new ways of understanding the roles we play."

~ Paula Carter, author of *No Relation*

"Laura Kroghoff's stories have the lyrical exhuberance of a Grace Paley in their bones."

~ Christopher Grimes, author of *The Pornographers* and *Public Works: Short Fiction and a Novella*

"In these beautifully written and disarmingly humane stories, Laura Krughoff points out the problems with our preconceived notions, and then imagines what new notions we might generate in their place so she can undermine those, too. Reading Krughoff is like having the nicest person in the world tell you there's no Tooth Fairy, but that, even if there were, said creature wouldn't act at all the way you'd think it would."

~ Andrew Farkas, author of *Sunsphere* and *Self-Titled Debut*

Laura Krughoff

Wake in the Night

 Arc Pair Press

ISBN-13: 978-0-9998453-8-7

Contents

ACKNOWLEDGEMENTS. The author would like to thank the following publications where these stories first appeared: *Washington Square Review* for "This is One Way," *qu.ee/r Magazine* for "History of a Hunting Accident," *Other Voices Magazine* for "Skinned," *Masque & Spectacle* for "By the Time You are One Hundred," and *Necessary Fiction* for "Wake in the Night."

This is One Way

Meet in high school, the Catholic kind. He is charming in that way boys can be, all hope and spirit and elbows. He is handsome enough, but not dashing. He comes from nothing. His father is famous for being a wonderful man who has never figured out how to keep his family fed. Keep company. This is the 1930s when people called it keeping company. Become bridge partners. Make a foursome with his best friend and your best friend who will marry right out of high school. Watch him fall in love.

Go away to college. Just for a year since it's all your father can afford. Get a glimpse of lives you'll never lead. Become popular. Learn that you are smart and beautiful and, though you can hide it well, cunning. Learn that these are all very good things. Go on adventurous dates with college boys. Let one take you up in an open cockpit airplane. Understand that the thrill is worth it even if the plane tumbles from the sky. Experience a sharp moment of disappointment when you land safely and have to continue with your own life, which will always feel quotidian after that. Date lots of boys. Date a few men. When you are home on weekends let him buy you sodas and ice creams on Saturday. On Sundays, after Mass, walk with him across town to the park on the river. Let him put a palm in the hollow of your back. Tell him about your other boyfriends. See the way he suffers.

Come home to your father's house and take a job as a clerk in a men's clothing store downtown. Love this job, the ringing of the cash register, the numbers in the ledgers, the feel of fine fabrics, the money rolled into tight tubes in your purse after you've taken your paycheck to the bank. Forget to think about all your college boyfriends. Forget to send them letters asking them to visit you out here in the sticks. Forget that your real job is the job of landing a husband until all your old boyfriends have vanished or been landed by someone else, someone half as pretty and smart as you are. Someone not cunning in the least. Discover that you no longer have any boyfriends with equal parts horror and disbelief.

He has been in Pennsylvania. He does something in business, something with sales. He has prospects. He's come home with an automobile, looking terribly handsome in his hat. Smile when you pass his pew on your way to Communion during Mass. The sight of you still makes his color rise. Stand on the steps in front of the church after service and ask him how in the world he has been. Look at him through your eyelashes. Say something worldly and knowing when he asks about you, something about your job and how a girl these days has to learn to take care of herself. Say something about the terrible dearth of decent men. Laugh. Know that this makes your eyes flash.

When he asks you to marry him, say yes, but only after he has finished paying for the automobile. Think, even in the moment you are walking down the aisle, that you would have chosen differently if you'd known it was time to choose. You're twenty-four and had hoped for years yet of enjoying yourself. Have a nasty row—not a lovers' spat— when he tells you you won't be able to keep your job at the clothing store. Say you love your job, you will not quit, it's absurd and there's no way he can make you. Listen, shocked, when he tells you that business here at home has dried up and you'll be moving back to Pennsylvania. Sit up all night, awake by a window in the living room of a house you rent in a town you'd never heard of in a state you'd never intended to live in, a cold, hard fear lying in your belly after having had a peek at his bank book. He has no money. You have no money. You have absolutely nothing and he refuses to allow you to have a job. Cry in fits of rage and frustration when you are alone. Sew your own clothes and even some of his. Tend his good suit as if your life depended on it. Invest in good gloves and treasure them. Be sure, always, that no one would ever know how poor you are when you attend Mass. You are beautiful and he is not bad looking, especially since you take special care to have his hat blocked, and good looks can conceal a lot. Pinch and save and stretch and do without. Resent that he never thanks you for the way you have sacrificed.

Have a baby. Watch in a postpartum stupor as he volunteers for the Navy. Do not believe him when he tells you it was the Navy or the draft. Go home to stay with your father. Feel dazed by your husband in his blindingly white dress whites when you see him off at the train station for his deployment. He's off to the Pacific. You've never seen the ocean. You do not understand this war. Tend your baby. Tend your father's house. Save every penny of the money he sends you. Recognize that he is sending you almost the entire sum of his monthly government check. Read his letters that speak of things you do not understand happening out on the vast ocean that spreads around him as empty and fearful as a desert. Try to compose letters to him but fail to. Fail utterly. Send a photograph of the baby when she turns one. Send another when she turns two. Go two and a half years without seeing him before he returns to the States for shore leave. You have plans to see him in New Orleans, but there is some absurd stroke of luck and the train he's traveling on will be passing through a town some seventy miles away en route to the south. The train will stop for forty-five minutes in the middle of the night. Go with his sisters, who adore him and who do not adore you, to meet him for a moment on that train. Take the baby who is not a baby anymore. Paint a big sign on a ruined sheet that says "Hello Vincent!" since you cannot think of anything else to say. Feel your heart in your throat when the train finally pulls into the station. It is a strange hour. People should not be awake, and yet the platform is teeming with women who have come for a glimpse of their men, just like you and your daughter and your husband's sisters have. You all hold up your sheet, but he doesn't come to greet you. His sisters shout for him. You drop your end of the sheet and board the train, moving from car to car, asking all these interchangeable men in their woolen blues if they know your husband. Some of them do. No one knows where to find him. Hurry from one car to the next. When the whistle sounds, run. Burst into compartment after compartment, no longer saying anything, just looking for your husband. When the whistle sounds again, hand the bottle of your husband's favorite bourbon, a bottle that cost you more than you spend on rationed flour and sugar and eggs and coffee in a month, to a boy you've never seen before and will never see again. He is so much younger than you. Step down onto the platform and find his sisters who are still standing with their slack sheet.

A week later, leave the daughter with his oldest sister and take the train to New Orleans. Feel like you are looking at a stranger when you see your husband. Something has happened to his teeth. They have rotted and begun to fall out. Tell him about the trip to the town seventy miles from your own and the baby and the sheet with "Hello Vincent!" written on it and his sisters and the bottle of bourbon. Refuse to cry. Smile and laugh when he tells you he fell dead asleep and slept right through it. In a hot hotel room in a strange and foreign city let him take your clothes off once you've gone to bed. Turn your face to the wall because of the way his ruined teeth affect his breath.

When the war is over, surprise him with all of the money you have saved. It is enough for a down payment on a house. You know the one you want. It is painted yellow and sits at the top of a hill. He has had his teeth pulled out and now has a good pair of dentures. He has a G.I. Bill. He is home from a good war and is offered a good job, a job that makes good money. Have another baby, a second girl. Wait to feel something. Expect to feel something that you don't. Have another baby, a boy this time, who is born too early and cries weakly for two days and then dies. Bury the third baby and wonder if this is what real grief feels like. It feels like being wrapped in yards of cotton batting and then being thrown down a well. Continue to save money carefully even though now you don't have to. Put aside money from your food and clothing budget to buy yourself luxuries—a silver tea set (which your children will eventually sell at a garage sale before you're even dead), calfskin boots, a fur coat (muskrat rather than mink, but it's better than just a stole). Shout at your husband when you're angry with him, which is most of the time. Slam cabinets and kick doors until he leaves without saying anything and takes his dinner and several glasses of bourbon down at the Knights of Columbus. Feel blinding fury when other women at church praise your husband and go on about how lucky you are. Conceal this. Bury it. Embalm it, at least. Have a fourth baby, another boy. This one lives. Tell your husband that's enough. He respects you. You count the days and pay attention to your cycle and if you say that he can't, then he doesn't. Spend a great deal of time feeling cheated, feeling denied, even though you are not sure of what.

Raise your children. The oldest marries young. You warn her about this. You caution her about marriage in general and her choice of this man in particular, but she'll hear none of it. She marries poorly and suffers for it, but it is out of your hands. Try to take pleasure in grandchildren but discover that you feel little for them. They are so messy and so sticky. You don't remember your own children being so sticky. Try to understand your second daughter. She is pretty and popular and plays the piano. But she is unhappy. She seems desperate and miserable most of the time. She graduates from high school and leaves home. She studies acting and literature and visits rarely. She becomes a hippie, or something like it. She wears her hair wild and dates all sorts of men. One of them is named Louie. Another is a black man. Eventually she comes home with one who rides a motorcycle and wears his thick, black, curly hair grown out in a bush around his head. He wears dark glasses, but at least he is white. You think he is white. Your husband likes him inexplicably. Your husband calls this daughter Butch, has since she was a small child, and the girl loves it. She calls him Pops. She calls him Daddy. Your husband has developed this close relationship with this daughter to spite you. She and her motorcycle-boyfriend sit out on the back patio with your husband, the three of them mixing drinks and laughing, while you cook. A dark part of your heart hopes this motorcycle-boyfriend will turn out to be a terrible person, just to teach your daughter and your husband a lesson, but he doesn't. He is a fine man and they eventually marry and they raise a passel of children who run wild and express themselves. The girls never learn to wear makeup. They play sports instead of the piano. You have long ceased trying to understand.

Somewhere along the way your son becomes an evangelical Christian. He comes home one day with his

Bible and tries to convert you. You tell him you are Catholic and your mother and father were Catholic and everyone in your family and your husband's family has always been Catholic and you don't need him coming into your kitchen telling you about Jesus Christ. He gets married and moves away and raises his children as far from you as possible. You have been refused almost everything you have ever desired. You tell yourself this in the dark at night. You nurse this wound. You come to love it.

The years pass. You are old now, but you don't know when that happened. You don't remember when it was that you lost your looks. You laugh with everyone else when one of the granddaughters finds a photograph of you from 1936 and says, "Grandma, you were beautiful," but it wounds you to the marrow. You are fat now. You are still exceedingly well dressed and never step foot out of the house without your makeup, but it has been decades since you were beautiful. Your husband ages, too, but men age differently. He still loves you. He still looks at you the way he did back in high school. You don't know why he still feels this way but he does. You wish, really, that he wouldn't. It makes him better than he deserves to be, and it makes you worse.

Your health fails first. There is a fall, of course. A stupid fall. You go down on the sidewalk in front of a restaurant like a doddery old fool and break your hip. It is humiliating to lie on the sidewalk until the ambulance comes. There is a rehab center and exercises, but you are never again as strong as you were once. You struggle in and out of chairs and even though you outweigh him, your husband learns how to lift you. He stands over your chair and you put your arms around his neck and he lifts you. "There you go, Billie," he says, using your family name. Your real name is Lucy Wilhelmina Josephine, but he has never in his life called you that. He brings you things you ask for. His sight is failing, but he counts out your pills every evening. After the hip, there is the Parkinson's and the high blood pressure and what your doctors call anxiety. You are probably dying, who wouldn't be anxious? He goes with you to every doctor visit. He holds doors open. He helps you in and out of the car. He is so accustomed to the habit of dressing well that he continues to even after you've ceased pressing his things and setting out which tie looks best with which shirt. Doctors and nurses praise him. Now that you are ill, he tends to you patiently. He tends to your every wish. Something wells within you when he bends over your chair and puts your arms around his neck. Something surges inside, filling your chest, compressing your heart, when you watch him counting out your pills and checking twice with the sheet the doctor gave him, which explains which pill is supposed to be taken when. Something happens when he guides you to your usual pew at Mass and then wheels your walker out of the way and helps you out of your coat. People see the way he takes care of you. You see the way he takes care of you. For the first time, you see him the way others seem to. He makes your heart flutter. You want nothing more than for him to sit next to you. You are flooded with something you've never in your life felt before.

You try to explain this to your second daughter one day. You say, "You know, I don't think I'd ever loved your father before now. I'd never truly loved him, but I do now."

"I don't want to hear that, Mom," your daughter says. "Good grief. What kind of thing is that to say? If that's how you feel, you can keep it to yourself." She walks away.

You are shocked. You want to explain, but she's not coming back to listen to you. She is thinking about all those years that have gone by, all those years and years and years since the two of you first met in high school, and she's thinking of them bitterly, and only with sympathy for her father, of course, but you're not talking about all those years. You're not talking about how you felt then. You're only talking about how you feel now. It is remarkable. You've never felt anything like it. That is all you'd wanted to say. You're not talking about then. You're only trying to talk about now.

History of a Hunting Accident

Did he hope to be a better man than his father? Did he promise himself to never be that stinking drunk, that raging husband, that fat man passed out in the kitchen? Did he blame his mother for how she kowtowed, how she ducked her head and bit her lip and twisted her apron strings? For how she apologized? For how she stayed?

Did he graduate from high school? When he landed that job at the grain elevators, a decent job making family wages, did he feel like a man at seventeen? Did his muscles stretch and harden beneath his work shirts? Was he a favorite of the other men, young and lean and hungry? Was he just a few years too young for Korea? By the age of twenty, had his skin begun to leather from the dust and chaff and the sun? Was he looking for a wife, after he bought that yellow house on Main Street, just down from the Bluebird Café where the farmers all gathered for coffee at six in the morning if the crops were in and not yet ready to be taken out? Had he started watching the pretty girls in their poplin dresses, who walked the sidewalks with ice-cream cones or sodas in those long summer hours of evening before dusk? He'd made a name for himself in that small town, rising above what his father had managed—did the girls notice?

Did he meet Jacob and Tobias at the grain elevators when they hauled in their father's field corn? Was it a friendship of half hours spent chewing and spitting tobacco back behind the silos, of three-word sentences about the sky and the weather and the price of wheat? Did Jacob and Tobias say that if he cared some time, he might could come to church? Did he squint his blue eyes over the grain wagons and parched earth and say, Maybe, though me and Jesus ain't had much business since my mama stopped taking me to Sunday school? When they laughed, was it good natured or uneasy?

How did he and Celesta first meet? Maybe Jacob and Tobias said he might as well come over for supper one night, have a good woman's cooking rather than always doing for himself? Did he say he didn't mind tinned beans and his own cornbread, but anyway, yes, he thought he just might? Did he go home to wash first, change his sweat-stained shirt and his Carhartts for something decent? Was he suddenly nervous when he parked his truck in front of the farmhouse way out at the other end of the county? Could he smell the beef and the noodles and the fresh bread from the porch? Could he hear Jacob and Tobias out in the barn with their father, discussing a heifer that might calve that night? Did something bitter and lonely turn over in his belly? When he went around back to greet the men, did he get a glimpse of Celesta through the kitchen window, or did he see her for the first time when all four of them came in from the barn together, leaving their boots in the mudroom? Did he know he would marry her when she looked up, her face flushed, from the pan of bitter lettuce she was wilting with vinegar and sugar and bacon fat?

Did his heart melt? Did his soul threaten to swim out of him, or did he simply think, yes, there she is, the girl I've been looking for? Did Jacob and Tobias see what was happening between him and their sister? Did they see

Celesta's eyes light, her pupils dilate, her hand reach for wayward curls, damp with steam from the boiling noodles? If they didn't see it, did their father? Did their mother? Or was love the last thing on their minds for Celesta, since she was only fifteen?

When they married at the courthouse six months later, just the two of them, secretly, did Celesta write a one and an eight on a scrap of paper and slip it in her shoe so that she wouldn't be lying when she told the judge she was over eighteen? What was she feeling as she stood there beside him, putting her life in his hands, swearing to honor and obey? What was she thinking? How thrilling was it, to throw off her childhood, to say yes, to quit school, to become a woman and a wife? Did her mother cry when he drove her out to the farm to deliver their good news? Did her father stammer, as gap-mouthed as a bass? Was it her brothers who first said congratulations, or did they, too, fail to be happy for them? Did her mother take her aside and say Celesta, when do you think you're due? Did Celesta say, Mama, I'm not pregnant, I'm in love? Did her mother say, Oh, girl, what have you done?

How long did the giddy bliss of washing his work clothes and cooking him dinner last? For how many months did her heart thrill at the mystery of him, this good-looking man, this hard worker, this serious and often silent husband? For how long did she wake with butterflies in her stomach at the thought of another day as his wife? Did she go out on the front porch of the yellow house with a cup of coffee on some mornings, after her husband had already left for the grain elevators, to catch her girlfriends as they walked to the high school? Did they stop and talk, clutch their books to their chests, turn their toes in saddle shoes with jealousy? Did she light a cigarette and sigh and say she would probably be pregnant before she knew it, and ask, with only the slightest hint of condescension, who was taking whom to prom? Did her girlfriends love her and hate her for how she'd leapt from girlhood to womanhood without them? Did Celesta revel in it, their jealousy and admiration? Would she rise from the porch steps and say, I better go in, I've got breakfast dishes to do, and I'm making a chocolate cheesecake for dessert tonight, who knows if it'll turn out right?

What kind of lovers were they? What did their skin and their sweat smell like? When it was over, who lay awake watching the other sleep? Was it Celesta? Was it him?

Was she more surprised than hurt or angry the first time he hit her? Did it come out of nowhere, that first time he popped her in the mouth, that first time she tasted the copper of her own blood? Did she stand in the living room, blinking, confused, touching her split lip and looking with an odd sense of wonder at the bright red staining her fingertips? Did she say, I'm sorry, please, I'm sorry, even if she didn't know what she was sorry for? Was he shocked and sorry, too? Was he the kind of man who swore he'd lost himself, he didn't know what had come over him, it would never happen again? Or was he the kind of man who left immediately, who went down the street to the Eagle Lounge and came home ready to pretend they hadn't fought, he hadn't struck her?

How long does it take love to sour? How did it happen for these two? What did he tell himself in his heart of hearts when he hit his sixteen-year-old wife? Hadn't he loved her? Hadn't his knees gone weak when she turned her pink face up to him? Hadn't she done everything he'd ever asked her to? In the kitchen? In the bedroom? Why did the world go white with fury when he looked at her? Why wasn't she pregnant? Who did she tell about him? What did she say when they went to her parents' house for Sunday dinner? What quiet words were passed between mother and daughter at the stove? How was her family planning to humiliate him? What would the whole town say when she packed her overnight valise and left him? Wouldn't they laugh? Wouldn't they say water finds its own level? Wouldn't they say he was just like his father after all? Why does she look at him like a deer caught in headlights every time he walks into a room? Why can't she see that that look on her face of terror and submission is what makes him want to break his knuckles on her cheekbones?

How long can she hide it? From whom? What does the doctor say the first time she goes in for stitches? What does he say the second? Does he say, Celesta, sweet girl, what are you doing to yourself? Or does he say, You're going to have to learn to be less clumsy? What does the nurse say? If the nurse says nothing, what do her eyes say? How frightened is it possible to be? What do you do when you discover that you've made an unfathomable mistake? What does her mother say when Celesta tells her everything? Does Celesta cry, or is she beyond tears? Is she in a land of fear and confusion that is beyond grief? What happens in her heart when her mother says, Try not to make him so angry? Does her mother say, Don't scorch dinner, or ask for money, ever, or nag him when he comes home from work? Does her mother say, Have a baby? Does she say, A baby sometimes makes everything turn out all right? Does she say, Don't tell your father, or the boys, it would eat them up? Does she say, He's young yet, sometimes it takes men a while? What is Celesta feeling as she drives herself home? What is she thinking?

How is Celesta's arm broken? Are the bones broken when he hits her, maybe with something heavy? Maybe when she raises her hands to protect her head? Or is her arm broken when he knocks her down, when she reaches out blindly to break the fall? What do they say to each other as he drives her two towns over to a hospital to have her arm set? Does he weep at the steering wheel? Does he say he promised himself he'd be a better man? Does he say it's not her fault, it's his, she's done nothing wrong? Does he say, with God as his witness he'll never raise his hand again? Does she say, Baby, I love you, please change?

Is it Jacob or Tobias who asks him to go hunting a year later? Is it doe season, or buck? Did Celesta pack apple butter sandwiches and a thermos of coffee for him before the sun was even up? Did she stand on the front porch, her bathrobe wrapped tight, waving as her husband disappeared up Main Street in her brothers' truck? How long had they been happy again together? Six weeks? Six months? Did he trust Jacob and Tobias? Did he feel his blood alive inside him as dawn broke over the horizon and he and Jacob and Tobias took their well-oiled guns from the rack behind the seats and slung them over their backs? Did they tramp across a harvested cornfield in silence, stalks and husks crunching under boots, the sky turning from indigo to robin's egg above them, their breath coming out in clouds? Did Jacob say they'd set up a deer stand in the trees down by the river where the ground was too wet to till? They were climbing a fencerow, weren't they, the two brothers in front, their sister's husband bringing up the rear? Did he see it coming, their betrayal? Did he see on their faces what they meant to do when they turned to him? Did he have time to panic? Did he have time to put his hands up? Or did the rifle go off as he glanced up at the morning sky, admiring the way clouds marbled the blue, feeling younger and stronger and happier than he had in a long time, thinking of his wife? Did their father know Jacob and Tobias were going to kill Celesta's husband? Surely Celesta didn't, did she? She loved him, for all his faults, she was besotted, still, wasn't she? Do the birds squawk or go silent when the rifle goes off? Does the man, shot through the belly, pitch forward or fall back? Does he writhe and groan, or does he die quietly? What do the brothers say in the still morning, their ears ringing with the rifle's report? Are they afraid of the coroner's assessment? Do they wipe down the rifle and try to position the body? Do they think about the angle of the bullet's entry, or do they know already that the certificate will list the cause of death as an accidental shooting, that the obituary will run on page two, after a page-one article about a tragic hunting accident? Do they consider the fact that their sister will examine the body later, will touch her husband's cold flesh, will mark the wound with her finger? Who stays with the body and who goes for help? What are they thinking? What are they feeling, other than the flood of adrenaline and the ache of their hearts in their chests?

Skinned

Erin and I had been out in her front yard trying to learn how to double-dutch. We'd been mesmerized by the whirling ropes of a group of black girls on *Sesame Street*. We were both ten and thought of ourselves as too old for *Sesame Street*, but my mother only let us watch PBS. As soon as the episode was over, we ran down to Erin's house and tied two double jump ropes to a persimmon tree out by the sidewalk so that one of us could turn and one of us could jump. Erin was having trouble getting the rhythm. She said I was turning too fast. I said she was jumping too slow. We were hot and uncomfortable in the early summer humidity. The cicadas were screeching away in the dogwoods and Erin and I were about to get into our first serious squabble of the summer when we heard thunder rumbling in the distance. We left the jump ropes lying across the sidewalk and sat on the concrete steps of her porch to catch a breeze while the storm blew in from the west. Soon the air felt cool and damp, the way my mother's hand felt against the back of my neck when I had a fever. When the sky split open with a hot flash of lightning and a deafening crack, we made a mad dash for the house. We watched through the screen door until the rain came down.

We could hear Erin's mother in the living room where

she seemed to sit all summer long smoking cigarettes and watching soap operas. Another clap of thunder drowned out the theme song to *Guiding Light*. Left to our own devices, after our front yard games grew dull, Erin and I always found ourselves looking for her three older brothers to tease. On that afternoon we checked the basement first, where Benji and Bobby sometimes sat watching their older brother, Jake, lift weights. When the boys weren't in the basement we knew to look for them up in the attic where Jake practiced the guitar and listened to records on an old turntable. I asked Jake once why he listened to music in the attic, and he said it was so his mother wouldn't bother him every five minutes, asking him whether or not he thought his albums were "appropriate." But I'd never heard Erin's mother bother any of her children during the daytime, at least, when the soaps were on. Sure enough, when we got to the top of the stairs, the hatch to the attic was open at the end of the hall, the rickety, fold-up ladder leading up into a dark, rectangular opening in the ceiling. Erin and I climbed up.

        None of the three boys noticed us. They were all gathered around the record player in the center of the attic, and Benji was showing his older brothers that he could do the moonwalk to *Thriller*. Benji was eleven, and a show-off in my opinion. He had the kind of face that was always red, as if he'd just been running. He never wanted to let Erin and me play with them no matter what the game might be. "But they're giiiirls," he'd say. Bobby, who was twelve, sat next to Jake, both the boys on over-turned crates. Bobby was wiry and quick to anger, and he liked to play games that started out as tag or keep-away, but he always modified the rules so every game ended up involving tackling. Jake was fourteen that summer. He had dark hair and dark eyes, like me, and I'd sometimes pretend that he was my brother instead of Erin's. He was too old to play with us, but he did sometimes anyway, telling Benji to give the girls thing a rest. He was doubled over with laughter watching his youngest brother moonwalk. Benji's socked feet slipped easily on the plywood floor. He slipped backwards with Michael Jackson's exaggerated steps, one hand holding an imaginary hat, one hand cupped over his crotch.

"What are you guys doing?" Erin asked when she got tired of feeling ignored.

"What's it look like, stupid?" Benji said. His face was flushed a brighter shade of red than usual due to the dancing and the attic heat.

"Come on in if you're coming, girls," Jake said. He leaned forward, elbows on knees, still laughing, and lit one of their mother's cigarettes. "Benji," he said, "I'm not shitting you, man. That was great."

Benji was mollified by his brother's praise and didn't bother complaining about the way Jake invited us to stay. We had listened to this record with Jake once before, and even though I wanted to stay, especially with the way Jake had smiled at us and said, Come on in, I was nervous about hearing the last song on the first side. I liked the record, mostly because Jake liked it, but the song "Thriller" gave me the creeps. I hated the howling wolves at the beginning and then the man laughing at the end. The song that Benji had been dancing to ended, then there was a moment of scratchy silence, and then the first wolf started in.

"Jake," I said. "Can we turn the record over? I like 'Beat It' better."

I could feel my heart rate picking up already and we were only a few bars into the song. I knew I was acting like a little kid, but "Thriller" scared me enough that I didn't care. Jake looked at me over the glowing tip of his cigarette as he inhaled.

"Fine by me," he said, and pulled the arm up, silencing the song. He held his cigarette between his lips while he turned the record over and lowered the needle again. Jake was always nice to me like that, and I appreciated the way he said, Fine by me, instead of making fun of me for being scared. In the silence before the first song on the second side started, I could hear thunder rumbling and rain coming down on the roof. I was glad I didn't have to hear that man laugh.

The attic was stuffy, the air scratchy with Jake's cigarette smoke, and humid from the rain outside. The only light source would have been a cramped, dirty window on the far wall, but because of the sudden summer storm the attic was dim and shadowy. The ceiling slanted sharply all the way down to the floor, and already Jake was too tall to stand up anywhere but in the middle. Soon Bobby would be, too. The cramped little room was crowded with boxes, old picture frames, broken lamps, trash bags full of outgrown clothes. In the very center, the boys had rearranged a couple of boxes and crates into something of a circle. Erin and I sat at the boys' feet. We listened to "Beat It" in silence. Jake smoked his cigarette and then stubbed it out on the floor. I was trying not to squirm or fidget or do anything that might cause Jake to ask us to leave, but I was sweating through my t-shirt in the attic's oppressive heat. My eyes had adjusted to the gloom, but the air felt almost too thick to breathe. My long hair clung, stringy and damp, to my forehead, my cheeks, my neck.

"What's the matter?" Jake asked.

"I'm hot. My t-shirt itches me."

"Then take it off."

I was about to follow his suggestion. The clingy cotton felt like more than I could stand, but Erin interrupted me before I could wiggle my arms out of the sleeves.

"She can't take her shirt off," she said. "She's a girl."

"Why's that matter?" I asked.

"Because girls aren't supposed to show their chests. It's nasty."

"Who says?" I asked. I knew women shouldn't take their shirts off. I knew girls had to wear theirs out in public, but this wasn't school or the grocery store. It was Erin's attic. At my house my mother still let Erin and me run through the sprinkler in nothing but our underpants, and that was out in the front yard.

"Everybody knows it," Erin said. "It's because girls have titties and boys don't."

"I don't have titties, and neither do you." This was true. We were ten years old and our chests were as flat and pink as her brothers' and they went around without their shirts on all the time.

"Not now, dummy," Erin said, "but we will."

"Oh, go ahead. Take your shirt off," Jake said. "Erin, stop being such a baby."

I looked at him. I looked at Erin.

"I'll give you a quarter," Jake said. He raised his eyebrows and smiled as if to say, I dare you.

I crossed my arms and took hold of the bottom of my shirt and pulled it over my head in one quick motion. Bobby's cheeks and the tips of his ears flushed a mottled pink that matched his younger brother's, but Jake just sat back, lit another cigarette, and exhaled a plume of blue smoke. The air that had, just moments before, felt stiflingly hot, now felt cool against my damp skin. I shook my hair because I liked the way it slapped against my bare shoulders. Nobody said anything, not Erin, not Benji or Bobby, not me. Jake just sat there with his eyes on me is if he were watching TV. I began to feel my heart pound, and I remember worrying that Jake would be able to see it, thumping away just beneath my flat chest. After a long moment he reached into his pocket and flipped a quarter at me. The gesture took me by surprise, but I caught it, and I was glad I hadn't flinched, hadn't closed my eyes.

"Take your shorts off," Jake said.

"Stop it, Jake," Erin said. And then to me, "Don't do it."

"I can if I want. Give me another quarter." I held an open palm out to Jake.

"Take your shorts off first."

"I'll tell," Erin said.

"Shut up. No you won't," Jake said. "Not unless you want to get us all skinned."

I knew Jake was right. Getting skinned was what they called it when their dad hit them with his belt. Erin and her brothers had a solemn pact that they'd never tell on one another if it meant that one of the boys might get skinned. Erin and I were watching TV the first time I heard the word used that way. Erin's mom was shouting in the kitchen, yelling at Benji to go to his room. Benji protested and then wailed at the top of his lungs as he stomped up the stairs.

"What's his problem?" I asked.

"Sounds like he's waiting for Dad." It was quarter after five. Their dad was due home in fifteen minutes.

"But why's he crying?"

"Cause he's gonna get skinned," Erin said. She looked over at me to see if I knew what that meant. "He's gonna get whipped with the belt."

"Do you get skinned?" I asked.

"No."

"Why not?"

"I'm a girl."

When Erin's father got home, she got up off the couch and turned the volume up on the TV.

I looked at Jake, but he just smiled casually, his eyes impassive, as if he didn't care whether I took off my shorts or not. The butterflies I felt in my stomach were new to me. I liked the way my body felt, skin tingly, limbs weak. I stood up and put my hands inside the waistband of my shorts. They slipped easily over my slim hips. I bent down to pull them over my feet, but I tipped forward with the motion, lost my balance for just a second, and had to catch myself with one palm against the gritty floor. I stood up, blushing from the awkwardness of the move. My legs felt long and bony, exposed all the way up to my underpants.

"Keep going," Jake said.

So I did. I slipped my underwear off. I kicked them free from my feet rather than bending down. I stood in front of Erin and her brothers completely naked, and the stagnant attic air seemed to swirl around my bare body. I had the tipping, shifting feeling of vertigo. Benji and Bobby stared at me, wide-eyed as if they'd never seen a girl naked before in their whole entire lives. Jake put his cigarette out on the floor and smiled.

"Nice," he said.

Erin stood up and left the attic without saying a word. I could hear her hands and feet smacking the rungs of the ladder on the way down. Jake tossed a second quarter at me, but this time I wasn't quick enough. The coin bounced out of my outstretched hands and clattered around on the plywood floor. I didn't stoop to pick it up. I just stood there, naked, meeting Jake's gaze, wondering if I should put my clothes on and go find out if Erin was mad at me or not.

"Benji, Bobby," Jake said, "get out of here."

The boys scrambled to their feet, ducked their heads when they passed me, and disappeared down the ladder. It was just me and Jake in the attic, and I wanted, more than anything, for him to say something nice to me. Instead he lifted the arm of the record player and switched off the machine. He leaned over, collected the two quarters from the floor, and put them in my hand. He chuckled under his breath, put his hand on my head and mussed my hair the way grandfathers do.

"We'll have to do this again sometime," he said, and then climbed down the ladder leaving me naked and alone in the attic.

Perhaps I should have felt shame, or anger, or betrayal at least. I know now that's what would have been expected of me, but I didn't know that then. What I felt, instead, was pride. I felt hot and electric on the inside. I had taken my clothes off and Jake had said, Nice, and the truth was his eyes on my body felt good. I took my time up there in the attic putting my clothes back on. I found Erin out on the front porch flipping through the glossy pages of her mother's *Cosmopolitan* magazine. She said she was tired of playing with me, that I should go on home. I knew she was mad, but I didn't care. I walked down the steps and did what I thought might be considered a saunter up the sidewalk until I was out of Erin's sight, and then I broke into a run, my new fifty cents jingling in my hand.

A week went by. I played at Erin's house almost every day. We worked on double-dutch out on the sidewalk. We played with dolls in her bedroom. We sat on the porch, trying to catch an afternoon breeze, looking at her mother's magazines. I tried to memorize the looks on the models' faces and the slouchy way they slung their weight back on one hip. I thought about what I'd done up in the attic with Jake almost all the time, while sitting at the dinner table with my parents, while examining my face in the bathroom mirror when I was supposed to be brushing my teeth. Mostly, though, I thought about the way the air felt on my bare skin while I lay awake through those muggy, early summer nights under the sticky weight of a thin sheet.

For a whole week I waited for Jake to ask me to take my clothes off again. I walked by the open door to his bedroom whenever I could, but he never called me in.

Benji and Bobby turned bright red every time they saw me, so I started sticking my tongue out at them. On a Tuesday afternoon, Erin and I were sitting at her kitchen table cutting paper dolls out of a book her mother had bought for us. We were trying to hurry up and finish before Erin had to leave for her ballet lesson. The dolls themselves were dressed in tightly laced white corsets and ruffley bloomers. I was cutting out the dolls, and Erin was cutting out their long dresses and parasols and bonnets. I thought they looked best without the fancy dresses, but I didn't say that to Erin. I had just started in on the last doll when we heard Erin's mother switch off the television in the living room. She walked into the kitchen with her sunglasses and car keys in her hand.

"Come on, hon, it's time to go," she said.

"Can I stay and finish, Mrs. Ross?" I asked. "I'll put the scissors away and go home as soon as I'm done."

"Sure, sweetheart," Erin's mother said, but Erin gave me one of her looks.

"Yeah, right," she said. I just blinked at her.

I heard the car doors open and shut and then the engine in their big Buick whine before it turned over. I heard the car back up out of the driveway and roll off down the street. The sound of the engine hadn't faded fully when Jake walked into the kitchen. He crossed to the refrigerator without looking at me, opened the door, pulled out the orange juice, and drank straight from the carton. Then he leaned against the counter and smiled at me.

"Hey, hot stuff," he said.

"Hey, yourself."

"You want to listen to some records with me?"

"Sure."

I didn't look at him. I played it cool. I worked the scissors around the curve of the final paper doll, careful not to cut in past the black line of her silhouette. I knew he was watching me. I let him wait. When the doll finally fell free, I stood up, swept the scraps into my hand, dropped them in the trash, and put the scissors where they belonged in the junk drawer next to the stove.

"I've got nothing better to do," I said.

We walked upstairs without talking. As we passed Benji and Bobby's room, Jake stuck his head in and asked if they wanted to listen to music. They looked at Jake, looked at me, nodded their heads. At the end of the hallway Jake pulled open the hatch to the attic and unfolded the ladder. We climbed up, Jake first, then me, then Bobby and Benji. Jake sat on a box, switched on the record player and put *Thriller*, the B-side up, on the turntable. He pushed a crate toward me, indicating that I should sit. Bobby sat next to Jake, and Benji sat across from me, bouncing one leg incessantly. We listened to "Beat It" without talking, all four of us watching our feet. In the silence between songs I could hear the needle turning in the empty grooves, the heavy sound of the boys' breath, and my own heartbeat. As the first notes of "Billy Jean" came up, Jake tapped my foot with his.

"Want a quarter?" he asked.

The way he looked at me wasn't different from the way he'd looked at me in the kitchen, or the way he'd looked at me, when he chose to, even before the previous week. It was as if he'd asked me if I wanted a Coke.

"It's fifty cents," I said.

Jake laughed, and I could hear Bobby shuffling his feet.

"And a quarter from each of them, too." I spoke only to Jake, indicating his brothers with a nod. As soon as I said it, a thrill ran through me. I felt in charge.

"I don't have a quarter," Benji said. He looked to his oldest brother as if expecting him to intervene. Jake looked at me with his eyebrows raised. His eyes were laughing, but his face was straight. "I don't—" Benji started again.

"Shut up, stupid," Bobby said. "I have a quarter."

"Go get it, then, and bring a quarter for Benji," Jake said. "Look on my dresser if you have to."

And Bobby scrambled to his feet, crossed the attic, and climbed down the ladder.

"Get a move on, kid," Jake called after him, and we could hear Bobby break into a run down the hall.

When he returned, he held out a quarter, two dimes and a nickel. I picked them up, one coin at a time, from his outstretched palm and put them in the pocket of my shorts. Jake fished in his pocket and held out two quarters. As I reached for them, he closed his fist.

"Maybe you could dance this time."

"Okay," I said.

I didn't know how to do that. What ten-year-old does? I just closed my eyes and listened to the music, tried to catch the beat of "Billy Jean." I thought it probably would have been easier if I'd been able to start at the beginning of the song. I kept my eyes closed so long the blackness behind my lids began to swim. There was only the music, only the hot, close air of the attic, only the rush of blood in my ears. When I began to feel dizzy, I started to wiggle, moving my hips the best I could, trying to think of the beautiful, seductive faces of the models in *Cosmopolitan*. Trying to dance and take my shirt off at the same time proved difficult. I got one arm stuck in the sleeve for a moment, the shirt half on, half off. My shorts and underpants were easier, although I stopped moving for a minute when "Billy Jean" was over. I froze until "Human Nature" started up, and then I slid my shorts and then my underpants down over my knees and kicked them off my feet. Once I was naked, I could feel the boys' eyes on my skin, even though I didn't open mine. I danced like that through the entire album, through "PYT" and then

"The Lady in My Life." I didn't stop dancing until I heard the scratch and thump of the needle at the end of the record.

I stood there in front of them, my chest heaving, trying to catch my breath. Jake snapped off the record player and put *Thriller* back in its jacket. I thought that he might say something then, but he just rubbed both his cheeks with one hand, his chin cupped in his palm. I pulled my clothes back on, then held out my hand for Jake's fifty cents. He dropped the coins, and they clinked together as I closed my fist. Then I climbed down the ladder into the bright light of the hall.

This became our routine. I would go to Erin's house on Tuesday and Thursday afternoons when her mother took her to ballet. Benji, Bobby, Jake and I would go up to the attic and listen to records. Jake always played the B-side of *Thriller*. I learned to anticipate the music, to recognize the rhythms, to know which way my hips were going to move. The boys would stack their coins on a box beside the record player, and after a song, or sometimes two, I would stand up and begin to dance. Sometimes, if I felt like it, I would not accept just a quarter from Bobby and Benji. I would make them go back downstairs to find more change, a nickel and a dime, maybe. I think Jake got into the habit of leaving pocket change on his dresser for this reason. If Bobby or Benji didn't return immediately he'd call down, "Check my dresser," and then whoever had gone in search of money would climb back up the ladder with the shiny coins in his sweaty hand. Sometimes, when the record was over and I'd put my clothes back on, Jake would say, "Get out of here, Bobby; hit the road, Ben," and his little brothers would obediently climb down the ladder and leave us alone.

On those afternoons, Jake would tell me to have a seat. He'd put another record on and light a cigarette and we'd talk. He'd tell me about searching through used record stores for an album he wanted to find. He'd lecture me about how cassette tapes were just a flash in the pan, how real music would always be on vinyl. Or he'd tell me about ninth grade, how stupid it was, how he sometimes got into fights.

"Who'd you fight?"

"Other guys, during lunch or after school sometimes."

"Why?"

"I don't know. They play football and I don't. That sort of thing."

Once, we talked about his father just a little.

"He's a mean bastard, but he's my dad, you know? I guess he's okay."

He talked to me as if we were friends, and then I didn't feel like just his little sister's dorky friend. It was nice up in the attic, but particularly nice on those days. A couple of times he picked up his guitar and played a little, and once I sat between his knees while he held the guitar across both our laps, and he tried to teach me a chord or two. I still played with Erin, but on those afternoons when she was at her dance class and I was up in the attic with Jake, I felt much older than she was.

On a white-hot day in the middle of July, Erin and I walked downtown to buy ice cream cones. The sidewalks were deserted in the midday heat, and we strolled leisurely, licking the ice cream that melted down our fingers and dripped from the bottom of the sugar cones. We could see all the grownups going about their grownup business through the cool plate-glass windows of the bank, the post office, the shops. They didn't take any notice of us, two little girls sweating in the summer sun. That was the way summer always seemed to be. The hotter the days got, the less attention anyone seemed to pay to a couple of girls in seersucker shorts and tank tops.

"I'm melting," Erin said, leaning against the brick wall of the bank, pretending like she was going to sink to the ground. "Let's go down to Jeanette's."

Jeanette owned a pawnshop in the basement beneath the sporting goods store. We had to go down the alley and around to the back to a set of concrete stairs that led down to her door. A hand-painted sign that said "Jeanette's Pawn and Jewelry" was bolted into the brick of the building just above the steps. Jeanette's shop wasn't air-conditioned, but down in the basement it stayed pretty cool, and she had an enormous industrial fan that stirred up the mildewy air. She was nice enough, and she didn't mind kids wandering into her pawnshop even if we rummaged around in boxes of comic books for hours without buying a single thing. The only problem was that her shop stank of stagnant water, mildew, and her own sweat. That and she might try to hug you if you got too close. She'd reach out one huge, meaty paw and catch you, pull you into a crushing embrace against her massive bosom. I often got caught by Jeanette. I would forget to pay attention and the next thing I'd know, I'd be smothered against the soft folds of her chest.

"Come on, don't be a baby. It's cool down there," Erin said. So we went.

Jeanette waved to us from her seat behind the gun counter, "Come on in, girls," then turned back to the magazine in her lap.

It took a minute for my eyes to adjust, going from the brilliant afternoon sun to the dim light of the basement pawnshop. I had to stand by the door and wait for the shadows in front of me to take shape. The jewelry part of the shop's name always seemed false to me. There was one locked case with three shelves of jewelry, mostly plain gold or silver chains of varying lengths, a couple watches, a handful of glass-stoned rings. The only truly impressive piece of jewelry in Jeanette's shop had been there as long as I'd known about the place. An engagement ring with a diamond that looked like a gumdrop. A curly, white-gold setting held the stone in place. Everyone in town knew that the ring had once belonged to the lawyer's wife, Mrs. Evelyn Hartman, and that she'd pawned the diamond when her husband left town with the girl who'd answered his phone as a part-time job through her last year of high school. Mr. Hartman and the girl were long gone before I was born, but it was the sort of scandal a town doesn't forget. Evelyn Hartman eventually moved to Florida to take care of her mother, but she left her beautiful engagement ring in the glass jewelry case at Jeanette's Pawn and Jewelry for the whole town to see. As far as I know, no one has ever bought the thing.

The rest of the basement was crowded with junk, lawn furniture, old coffee tables, garden tools, chain saws, ceramic lawn ornaments, kitchen appliances. The shelves along the walls were crammed with broken speakers, needleless record players, rusting trumpets, unstrung guitars, and a black-and-white television with a fine crack in the glass. Boxes of magazines, memorabilia, and collectibles piled up in the corners. The gun case took up most of the far wall of the shop. Handguns, pistols, and old revolvers lay on the top two shelves, shotguns and rifles on the third. The gun case was lit with long fluorescent tubes, and the weapons seemed to glow in the bluish light. Even the old guns marked "antique"—the word printed in black marker on an index card—seemed recently oiled and fully functional. The gun case was the bread and butter of Jeanette's pawnshop, and she sat behind the long counter like a fat old badger.

Erin saw the bike first. I was busy in a corner flipping through a box of dusty records, looking for ones I thought Jake might like. When I looked up, Erin was standing in front of the bike, stroking the streamers on the handlebars. It was a Huffy girl's bike with a purple banana seat. The frame was clean white with three pale, purple roses painted on the top crossbar. The handlebars, silver and shiny, were not even a little bit rusted yet. The bike looked brand new. The look on Erin's face told me she wanted the bike. She already had one, but it didn't have a banana seat. Her parents had given her a blue Schwinn for her birthday the summer before. I didn't have a bike. When Erin and I wanted to ride together, I had to borrow Benji's, but I knew my parents wouldn't buy the bike for me. We'd celebrated my birthday at the beginning of May, and Christmas was months away.

"How much do you want for the Huffy?" I asked Jeanette. She looked up from her magazine, squinted over toward Erin and the bicycle.

"Twelve bucks," she said.

"Will you hold it for me?"

"How long?"

"Till the end of summer. I'll buy it before school starts."

Jeanette looked at me. I could see her calculating in her head, weighing the probability of me actually coming back to buy the bike. I could feel Erin's eyes on me as well, both jealous and incredulous.

"Why not?" Jeanette said.

"Promise?"

"I said I would, okay?"

We stayed in the pawnshop for a few more minutes, then climbed the cement steps back into the sunshine. I felt like sneezing from all the dust and mildew in the basement, and from the brilliance of the sky. Erin and I both squinted and shaded our eyes. We walked a couple of blocks before she said anything.

"How are you going to buy that bike?" she asked.

"I've got money," I said.

"No you don't."

"Yes I do."

"Prove it," she said.

"It's in my sock drawer at home. I'll show you."

"Well, where'd you get it?"

I knew it wouldn't do any good to lie to Erin. I never could. Sometimes we pretended that we could read each other's minds, and sometimes, like just then, it felt as if we really could.

"Come on, tell me," Erin said. "You have to."

"Your brothers. They give me money."

Erin kicked a broken piece of glass off the sidewalk and into the gutter.

"I don't think you should do that anymore," she said.

"Why not?"

"It makes you a slut."

"What's a slut?"

"A girl who likes to do it with boys," she said.

I waited for her to go on. I knew enough to know I was being insulted, but I didn't know exactly how.

"You know what 'do it' means, don't you?" she asked.

She knew already that I would have to say no. I shook my head and continued to wait.

"It means get naked, stupid. A slut is a girl who likes to get naked with boys."

I thought about this as we walked. I turned the word over in my head. Slut almost sounded nice in some ways. Slut was the kind of word you'd get in trouble for using, which made it exciting to say. I liked thinking that there was a dirty word that could be used to describe me. I didn't yet know that I was supposed to spend my whole life making sure that there wasn't.

"Yeah," I said at last, "I think I'm a slut."

I continued to strip for Erin's brothers twice a week while she was at ballet. I didn't feel sad that Erin didn't play with me as much since that afternoon at the pawnshop, that sometimes she wouldn't play with me at all for days at a time. I traded our friendship for the way Jake made me feel up in the attic, his eyes warm on my body, his mouth turned up just slightly in a friendly smile. I had a shrink once, many years later, who called Jake a predator, tried to make me a victim of something. But I could have kept my clothes on if I'd wanted to. I didn't.

I was pulling on my clothes on one of those days when Jake sent Benji and Bobby away. I had taken to the habit of turning my back to Jake when I was dressing, a small gesture toward modesty that strikes me as silly now. I had my shorts on, but not my shirt, and when I glanced back at Jake he was looking at me. He sat slouched forward with his elbows on his knees and his chin in his hands, just watching me. I'd never noticed him watching me put my clothes back on before.

"Come here," he said.

I walked over and stood in front of him. Sometimes I felt a little foolish in his presence with my clothes back on, and this was worse, standing in front of him half-dressed. He reached out and put his hands on my hips. His hands felt hot on my skin, even through the cotton of my shorts. He hadn't put a new record on yet, so the attic was completely quiet.

"You're pretty, you know that, kiddo?" he asked.

I didn't trust my voice, so I just shook my head.

"You are," he said. "I think so."

He pulled me to him, the weight of his hands making my knees weak. I didn't know what to expect. I didn't know what would happen next. All I knew was that I felt lightheaded when he raised one hand and put it at the base of my neck. I wondered for a split second if I were going to faint. He pulled me down toward him until my face was close enough to his that I could feel his breath on my lips, and then he kissed me. His mouth was warm and soft on mine, and he just held it there at first. Then he opened his lips and in the contact of our mouths together, I opened mine. I remember feeling as if I were suddenly suspended in a vacuum, as if nothing else existed except the hot darkness around us and the damp heat of his mouth on mine. He put his tongue between my lips, slipped it over my teeth, and then he pulled me so close that our whole bodies were touching and his tongue was deep inside my mouth. His tongue filled up every inch of space between my teeth. I felt as if I were disappearing. I felt as if there were nothing left but the slick, strange, slipperiness of that first kiss.

He pushed me back and let his hands drop. We didn't say anything for a long while. Finally, he leaned back and I sat Indian-style on the floor between his knees and we looked through his record collection together, each of us blowing dust off the jacket covers. He leaned over me, one arm draped casually over my chest, and in that moment, I felt closer to him than I'd ever felt to anyone in my whole life. I thought how nice it would be if he'd always sit with me like that, if he would always take care of me.

"Erin says I'm a slut."

I said this before I realized I was going to. It wasn't something I'd planned. But once the word was out there, I was glad I had. I wanted him to know that I was old enough to talk about what we were doing, that I wasn't just some dumb kid who didn't even know what a word like that could mean. Jake's reaction surprised me.

"What did you say?" he asked, turning me around to face him.

"I said Erin says I'm a slut. Because I do this. I'm probably even more of a slut now that I've kissed you."

Jake had me on my feet before I knew what was happening. He was suddenly years older than me again. His hands were strong, the way grownups grip a child when they're angry. Even though I was standing and he was sitting, he felt much bigger than me. We were in the exact same position we'd been in when he pulled me down and kissed me, but this time I felt like a little girl in his hands.

"You're not a slut," he said. "You're not a slut, and don't let anyone say that you are. If someone says that to you, ever again, I'll take care of it."

"Is it that bad?" I asked. I felt that prickly tightness in my throat that meant I was going to cry, and I didn't know why. "I mean, it's that bad? I told Erin I thought I was."

"Yeah, it's bad. Or people think it's bad, or something. But the thing is you're not one, okay?"

"Okay."

I wasn't crying yet, but I knew I would be soon.

"Go home, kiddo," he said.

"I'm sorry. I didn't mean—"

"Just go home." He wasn't looking at me anymore. He had his head in his hands.

I would have gone home if I'd had the chance. I would have pulled on my t-shirt and climbed down the ladder and, most likely, Jake would have never asked me to listen to records again. I stood for a moment watching him in the attic. His dark hair curled at the base of his neck and behind his ears. I noticed a pimple in the soft spot behind his jaw. I remember feeling a deep sense of loss in that moment, knowing that he would never really look at me again, but maybe I only remember things that way now. I know that my throat still itched, and I would have said something to Jake but I knew that the next time I opened my mouth I would cry. I had just picked up my t-shirt when we heard heavy footfalls in the hall and then Jake's father shouting up the ladder at us.

"Jake!"

Jake's head snapped up in my direction, but he was looking through me, his dark, panicked eyes on the open hatch.

"Jake!" his father called.

The color drained from Jake's face, and it seemed that I could see him shrinking, his broad shoulders and strong arms growing thin beneath his shirt, his frame folding in at the chest. He opened his mouth but no sound came out. We could hear his father's hands and boots on the rungs of the ladder, and I felt dizzy and disjointed, as I feel sometimes in my dreams. And then Jake's father hoisted himself up into the attic, huffing from anger and exertion. He was a large, red-faced man with thick lips and close-set eyes. He carried his weight cinched up above his belt, and I had sometimes wondered how his legs held up all that bulk. There was no room for a man his size in the attic. He should have been at work. Even if he had come home in the middle of the afternoon for some reason, he would have never come up to the attic. Erin had told on us. There was no other possible explanation. In Erin's eyes I had done something terrible enough to warrant her brother getting skinned. Jake would get it from his father, but Erin, I knew, had told on me.

"You want to tell me what the hell's going on up here, son?" Jake's father asked. I was standing between the two of them, but Jake's father looked right through me, just as Jake had.

"Dad," Jake said. "I… we… it's just," but he couldn't make any more words come out. His voice was high and his breath shallow, and I knew that if I didn't get out of the attic I was going to see Jake cry. He stayed sitting, crouched over, his hands buried between his thighs, and there was something terrible about the way his neck looked, his head twisted around to look up at his father. Jake's father unbuckled his belt and pulled it free of the loops on his pants. Once he had his belt off, folded back on itself in his hand so that the buckle and the free end smacked together, he looked at me for the first time. He looked like the sight of my thin shoulders and flat chest was enough to make him sick.

"Put your goddamn shirt on," he said. His voice was a freight train. His voice could have knocked me flat.

Getting into my t-shirt with Jake's father looking at me was the most difficult thing I've ever done. I couldn't make my arms move the right way. I couldn't get the shirt straightened out. Only later, at home, did I discover that I had my t-shirt on backwards and inside out. Jake's father took me by one arm, his rough hand pinching the skin under my armpit, and lifted me out of the way.

"Stand up, you little fucking pervert, and take it like a man," he said, but Jake didn't move. I should have gotten out of there as fast as I could, but I stood, frozen, and watched the belt cut through the air and crack against Jake's back twice before I clambered down the ladder and ran home.

I went to Jeanette's to buy the bike that same afternoon. I didn't know what else to do. I counted out twelve dollars in quarters and tied the coins up in a handkerchief. I walked the six blocks to her pawnshop alone, even though I wasn't supposed to go that far without Erin. We were supposed to be on the buddy system whenever we left our own yards. Jeanette seemed to have forgotten that she'd promised to hold the bike for me, but it was still there in the pawnshop all the same. The bike was just as beautiful as it had been the first day I saw it with Erin. Part of me had hoped that it wouldn't be, that it would be rusted and ruined, that the tires would be flat, or at least that I wouldn't still want it. But I did. I wanted that bike more than I'd wanted it before, and my hands shook as I untied the handkerchief and spilled the mountain of coins out on the glass top of the gun counter. We made piles of the quarters, each one four coins deep. When we had counted out the twelve dollars, Jeanette raked one arm across the glass and drew the coins into a tin box that she kept at her feet. It was not easy for me to carry the bike up the stairs all by myself, but by lifting the front tire one step at a time, and resting my shoulder against the handle bars, I managed to get the bike up into the alley. A breeze lifted and fluttered the purple streamers before I even got on and pedaled for home.

      The air rushed past me, and soon the houses on my quiet street whizzed by, one right after the other. The muscles in my legs began to burn. I could feel the heat, too, in my chest. When I reached my house I stopped in the front yard just long enough to tug off my clothes, strip down to nothing but skin. I kicked off my sandals, my shorts, my underpants. I pulled my t-shirt over my head in such a hurry I heard one of the underarm seams rip. I left my clothes in a pile on the grass. I couldn't have said why I yanked my clothes off then. I know now that when I stripped down in my front yard on that August afternoon, it was a young girl's last-ditch effort to get her pride back. To prove nobody else could make me feel ashamed. What does a girl know about things like that? I got back on my bike and pedaled for all I was worth. I rode that bike furiously, hit top speed by the time I passed Erin's house. She was sitting on the top step of the porch. I rode by too fast to register how she was looking at me. I wanted to be a flash of pink skin, flying hair, whipping streamers. I wanted to be the fastest, most furious, naked, ten-year-old girl to ever ride her bike through our neighborhood.

By the Time You are One Hundred

By the time you are one hundred, you have buried almost everyone you have ever loved. One would think death and dying would be familiar to you now, after all of these years of outliving. And yet each death is its own surprise. Each death is as singular as the first you can remember, your mother's, when you were twelve. You remember little of her illness—pregnancy, a difficult birth, septicemia, an infection that turned her nail beds blue. You were sick with scarlet fever that winter. When the doctor came to the house to see the both of you, he told your father you were more likely to die than your mother was. You lived. Your mother didn't. She delivered her last daughter on Christmas day and was dead before the Epiphany.

You were still so ill. Your father carried you into the parlor after your mother died, after her body had been washed and dressed and the soiled linens of the sick bed had been stripped. He wrapped you in a sodium bromide–soaked sheet before lifting you to his chest. He was a farmer, an often failing farmer, but a farmer nonetheless, and he could lift a calf or a colt so he had no trouble lifting you. You have an hallucinatory memory of your mother's dead body, of being told to kiss her cold lips. You thought your father was going to put you in bed with the body. You wondered if you, too, might be dead. Your nightclothes were soaked through with sodium bromide. You shivered. Your own fever burned. Here was your dead mother. Death seemed pleasant enough if it turned out to be simply a dark room, a stripped bed, a cool body, and quiet.

You lived. As did the baby your mother died birthing, though that, too, was uncertain for a while. A German woman in your parish had a recipe for making formula. You do not remember the recipe now, but it involved boiling flour and other ingredients wrapped in cheesecloth until the flour turned into a brick and then grating and dissolving the boiled flour in scalded sheep's milk. Still the baby suffered and cried after each bottle. Still she remained all head and huge eyes and spindly, brittle limbs. For one year you and your older sisters worked to keep that baby alive. She was dear to you. You loved her fiercely. She did not die. You did not let her.

Though your little brother was thrown through the glass windshield of a Model T the following summer and had his throat slit, he did not die either, which was a relief since your brother's death would have been the end of your father. There is grief that can be born and there is grief that cannot. He had five daughters and one son. Your little sister, Mildred, was in the automobile with your father and brother at the time of the accident. She remembers—still, she is not dead, she is ninety-eight and blinder than you are and you speak on the telephone once a week—your father crying, "My God! My son!" cradling the boy in the dirt. He was stitched up. He was fixed. You and your sisters loved your brother for that, for not dying in your father's arms.

Your sister Gertrude—Gertie—was the next death. Tuberculosis of the spine. You've asked doctors in the years since if that is possible, tuberculosis of the spine, or if that's something old-time doctors made up. They say it is possible. Even now. The condition exists. The bones grew in on themselves. She gnarled up like a stunted tree and her chest narrowed. The doctors wanted to operate, to put a steel rod in there, to force her spine to go straight. She was frightened. She said, "Please, no, Father. I don't want it. Don't let them operate." Eventually there was no room left inside for her lungs. You still miss her. Later—not yet, but later—you will think she has come to visit you. You will think Gertie has come to visit. Which is surprising since you were always so much closer to Mary, the baby. You were twelve and had a baby. You and Gertie and your oldest sister, Dorothy, had a baby. Mildred was too young to help. But Mary does not pay ghostly visits, not even at the very end.

But it is life you think of at one hundred. It was life you thought of, shopping with a great-niece for your one-hundredth-birthday party. You dress smartly, pants suits and sweater sets and skirts with blazers, but you wanted something special for your party. A dress. You bought a pale green dress that shimmered gold in the right light. Leonard loved you in green. The great-niece told every sales clerk at Von Mar that you were one hundred, as if she had something to do with it, but you are not embarrassed, not at this age, not looking and feeling as good as you do. You do not feel old. You simply feel as if you have lived a very long time.

You had fifty-three years with Leonard. Fifty-three years you spin out in your memory, sometimes, lying in bed on nights when you do not sleep. Each one of those years a blessing in the living of it and a blessing in the remembering. You were Depression-era sweethearts. You were working in the Tea Room at L.S. Ayers when you met Leonard. You loved being a working girl: the bustle of the department store, the clamor of city streets, the paycheck at the end of the week. You rented a room from a widow who lived six blocks from downtown, and you could come

in as late as ten o'clock on a Friday night. There was plenty
of time to go to the cinema with a friend who worked in
linens. She said her fellow had a friend in town. She said the
cinema would be more fun as a foursome. She asked if you
wanted to come. You said yes.

You hoped he would love you from the moment you
saw him in profile, smoking a cigarette under an awfully
nice hat. He looked at you sidelong. He had wicked eyes.
He could smile without moving his lips. You knew if you
married him you would always laugh and laugh. You
bought your own silver plate from L.S. Ayers when you
and Leonard married. You expected no wedding presents
and you received none. You wore blue on the day you were
married, blue for fidelity. You saw no reason to bother with
a dress you couldn't wear again and white made you feel
like a frosted cake. Leonard bought you a diamond years
later once he had a job with Campbell's Soup, but first there
were the lean years and then there was the war and his stint
in the Navy—the years without him one long black night,
the radio crackling on the kitchen table, coffee burning in
the stove-top percolator. Even those years you remember
without bitterness. You were a lucky wife. Your husband
came home. Not just in body but in spirit.

Fifty-three years with that long-faced practical joker.
Fifty-three years with his strong hands and his good fashion
sense and his whiskey neat and cigarettes. Twenty-three
years before him. Fifty-three years with him. And now,
almost twenty-five years again without him. That is what
surprises you. You felt older on your first day as a widow
than you feel now. Who would have thought you could
have lived this extra life without him? You would not have
thought you would have wanted to. Thank heavens that our
young selves are not allowed to tell us how to live our old
age. Our young selves know nothing. You miss Leonard,
but you have loved these nearly twenty-five years—these

twenty-four years and counting. You still love this long, strange life.

You have buried your stepmother and your father, who lived to be one hundred and four. You buried Dorothy, who dropped dead of a stroke at sixty, which only sounds old to those who don't know any better. You tell anyone who will listen that the sixties are the best decade. By sixty, you had raised your child—you had one, a son, Leonard's nephew whom you adopted—and had worked the longest and hardest years of your life. You were old enough to know what pleasure was and young enough to enjoy it. Because you were lucky, your marriage had burrowed its roots so deep into both of you that you and Leonard were like two great limbs on one stout trunk. You think of Leonard from all the years of your life, but most often, from when you were both in your sixties. Your bodies settled and solid. Your faces creased but not yet deeply lined. You think of him sitting in a wicker chair out in the Florida room of your place in Sarasota, reading the paper, looking up as you bring out afternoon cocktails. "Hello, bird," he says. He sets the newspaper aside and lights a cigarette. "Hello, love," you say and he pats your knee.

You do not think of Leonard's death. What is there to think of? Emphysema. Lost breath. His flesh wasted down to papery skin and spare bone. His move from the bed you'd shared for all the years of your marriage to the recliner in the living room. Oxygen tanks. Little sips of breath. Mary came to you then. She came to you with her own thin frame and her beautiful face, having buried her last husband. She had had several of them, some of whom she might not have technically married. But Frank Pollard was a good man, and he loved your sister. When Mary buried Frank, she called and said, "Pauline, I'm moving in with you. Don't say a word. I don't want to hear it." And she did move in, unpacking her suitcase in the guest bedroom, leaving her dentures in a glass by the bathroom sink at night. "I'm here to help," she said. "I've been to this vaudeville show." She cooked and cleaned and answered letters and the telephone. For the last six months of Leonard's life you didn't have to think about anything. You and Leonard simply sat together and talked, out on the balcony when the sun was shining, in the living room all through sleepless nights, a blanket pulled up to his impossibly narrow chest. When he could not talk, you simply sat together. You breathed. He struggled to. Mary boiled chicken and rice and made you eat. Mary told you when three days had passed so you knew when to take a shower. Mary made a hair appointment for you once a month and she sat with Leonard and held his hand every minute you were away. Leonard died in the middle of the night. Mary knew, even though you didn't cry out. You didn't make a sound. She came out of the guest bedroom in her housecoat and slippers. You were stroking Leonard's yellow face, the last few wisps of his hair. You kept putting your hand to his chest to see if you could feel anything stirring inside him even though he hadn't moved, hadn't blinked, in half an hour. Mary sat on the davenport. You were alone with your dead husband, but your sister was there. "I didn't know," you said, finally. "Of course not," Mary said. "I couldn't have known," you said. "No," Mary said. "A husband is different." His eyes were glassy. He was a body. Just skin and hair and bone. "I don't want to kiss him," you said. "You don't have to," Mary said. "Will you phone John?" you asked. "Of course," Mary said.

Mary never moved out. You had five delightful years of being old ladies together. Those years were wonderful. You crocheted blankets for everyone you could think of—your son and his wife, your grandchildren and great-grands, your nieces, your nephews, all of their children. You painted ceramics and sewed dresses out of outrageous Lili fabrics. As a joke, you sewed matching jumpers for the two of you and for your sister, Mildred, who'd been a nun since she turned nineteen. You wore them for a holiday party one year, the three of you dressed like aging triplets. You and Mary spent the winter months at your home in Florida. You bought brightly colored swimsuits. "We look like ridiculous birds," Mary said. "Look at our plumage." She was a blue heron. You were more of a chickadee. "We look like over ripe tropical fruits," you said. You wore linen shirts and floppy hats against the threat of skin cancer, but you stuck your wobbly, marbled legs out in the sun. The sun felt so good. You couldn't help yourselves, and you loved those old legs of yours anyway. You swam laps while Mary sat in a lounge chair smoking cigarettes and reading magazines from behind amber sunglasses. You rested your chin on the tiled edge of the swimming pool and watched your glamorous little sister exhaling clouds of smoke. "You are going to die like Leonard," you said. She would have been diagnosed with emphysema already if she had only gone to the doctor. You both knew it. "Yes," Mary said. "That's unkind of you," you said. Mary laid her magazine in her lap but she did not stub out the cigarette. "I know," she said. "I could go somewhere else. When it's time. I could go off somewhere to die. You shouldn't have to do this twice." You shielded your eyes from the sun with one hand. You said, "I dragged you into this world, Mary Agnes. And I'll be damned if you go somewhere else to leave it." Mary nodded. "Okay," she said. "I'll stay."

Every Sunday you went to Mass. Mary went shopping. She hadn't stepped foot inside a Catholic Church since your father and stepmother brought her back from the Magdalene Home at sixteen. She was pale, and silent, and furious, her breasts still leaking. You never spoke of that time. Neither of you ever did. You never knew if Mary knew that you and Leonard went to speak to the mother superior of the Magdalene Home to see about adopting the baby. You had been married long enough to know that you were not going to have one on your own. You wanted that baby as if you, yourself, were pregnant. You wanted Mary to live with you and Leonard instead of going to the home, but your father and stepmother would hear none of it. The mother superior said it would be best for the baby if it had a fresh start, if it were adopted by strangers, if it didn't have its past lurking in the family. Leonard went to talk to your priest, but he said the same thing. You don't know if Mary's baby was a boy or a girl. You don't know if she ever held it. But Mary never went to Mass again and she never had another baby, even after all those husbands. When she was very close to the end, wheezing, even with oxygen, sleeping sitting up in the recliner Leonard died in, Mary said, "You can have a Mass if you want to. For my funeral." The two of you were watching *Jeopardy*. You both had a crush on Alex Trebek. You looked at Mary. Her skin was the color of pewter. "I know it matters to you," Mary said. "It does," you said. "I don't know anything about my soul," Mary said, "but if you can get a priest to say it, I think a Mass would be alright." Your priest was a kind man. He came at the very end and Mary let him give her the Last Rites. She didn't go to her maker as a stranger. She went like the child she was, wasted down to the same huge head and wide eyes she started with.

You rented a little apartment in a retirement community close to your brother and his wife. He had a daughter and her family close by. Leonard's niece and her family lived close, too. At ninety, you decided to stop driving. You visited your son and his wife in Virginia once a year. By then John's children were long grown, of course, the boys with children of their own, although neither married his children's mother. You wished John would do something about that, but you didn't interfere. You just loved them, a grandmother's prerogative. And John had his own hard row to hoe before becoming your son. You don't remember how the boy's mother died, maybe cancer, some long, sad illness. But you do remember the day his father died in a car accident. John was nine, the poor thing. He came to live with you, at first splitting his time between you and Leonard's sister's family. When he was ten, John asked you to adopt him. It was summer and he was out of school. He was trailing after you, asking ten thousand questions when all you were trying to do was dust the living room and set out the tables for a card party that night. "Why haven't you had any children, Aunt Pauline?" he asked. You sprayed Pledge on an end table. "Sometimes two people just don't," you said. "Uncle Leonard and I wanted to have children, but we just weren't able to." The child was silent for a moment before he asked, "Have you ever thought of adopting one?" You dusted the lampshade. You could feel your face flush. "Yes. We have thought of that." John began to rearrange the pictures arrayed on top of the television. "Have you ever thought of adopting me?" he asked. "Would you like that?" you asked. John nodded, solemnly."Let's talk to Leonard," you said, and John was your son before school started. "He has been a good son to me," you say, when you are much older, when you look back. After John died the day you turned ninety-eight, you say, "He was always a good son to me."

John's death is the only death you cannot look at with anything but bitterness. "A mother should not bury her son," you say. You do not celebrate your ninety-ninth birthday. You are still grieving. By the time you are one hundred, the pain is not so searing, not so fresh. Pragmatically, you understand that at seventy-six John had lived the life most men are allotted, that he was too old to have died young. But this does not change the fact that when a son dies before his mother, that son has died too young. Such loss should not be suffered. Not by anyone.

You are tired of all this dying. Your brother died a year after his wife. Your cousins all died, various more distant relatives. When Phyllis, a favorite cousin from your childhood, died, her friend Linda traveled home with the body, sat with the family at the viewing and everything. Phyllis and Linda had been dear friends for ages and had lived together for years in a little house outside Boston where they were both professors. You suppose they must have been lovers. That had not occurred to you until the funeral. At the funeral you felt enormously sad for Linda. To have always been a friend and not a wife. The world is so much stranger than you ever thought it could be. You see that now. That is what comes from a long life. Not wisdom but wonderment. Perhaps wonderment is what keeps you going. You are a like a clock with all its gears oiled. There seems no reason for you to stop and you are curious to see what will happen next.

At one hundred, you do twenty minutes of exercises in bed every morning. You stretch. You point and flex your feet. You do leg lifts followed by arm lifts. You eat sensibly and walk one mile every day and take naps in the afternoon. You listen to books on tape and visit with friends you've made in the retirement community and watch the news, although it often alarms you. You telephone Mildred once a week at the convent. You will not bury Mildred. You simply refuse. Everyone else calls Mildred Sister Noel Marie, the name she chose when she entered the order, but you still call her Mildred. You might be the only person on the planet alive who knew her when she was Mildred. You celebrate holidays with your nieces, and your son's widow visits, and though almost everyone you have ever loved has died, you are not alone. You are tired of death, but you are not tired of living. Each day something new happens.

During the summer of 2010, the summer you are

one hundred, you become transfixed by the Chilean mining accident that traps thirty-three men. You learn about the accident first on the nightly news and then you switch over to CNN. You call Mildred to tell her about it, about the explosion and the collapse and the discovery of the thirty-three men so terribly trapped. You cannot imagine what the men must be experiencing—the darkness, the bad air, the weight of all that rock and dirt above them. You see on the news how a tent village of wives springs up at the mouth of the mine. You find Chile on a map in the library. It is a long curl of a country. You've hardly ever thought about Chile before in your life, but now you think about Chile almost all the time. NASA sends a team of experts to assist. You are riveted. The summer drags on with the men still buried and you begin to wonder how it will all end. Your nieces explain things you don't understand. They follow the accident with you so that when you have questions they can answer them.

You don't know what it is about this accident. You have lived through the twentieth century. There have been catastrophes around every corner in world history. Thirty-three men buried in a mine in some remote corner of South America is hardly the worst thing you've ever heard of, but you can't stop thinking about them. You can't stop thinking about their wives. Their children. Finally, in October, the experts say it is time to pull the men out. You stay up to watch the rescue on television. Night falls around you. You forget to turn on lights. Soon it is just darkness and the flicker of the television. You feel like the only person awake in your retirement community, maybe in your town, maybe in your whole time zone. You are alone, in the deepest watches of the night, witnessing the earth broken open, waiting for thirty-three men to be pulled out. Something happens when the first man is finally extracted. He is not a mining-accident survivor. This is not a rescue. You've all been mistaken. Men don't live that long in the belly of the earth. This is not a rescue. It is a resurrection.

You have lived to the end of time. The graves are open and the dead are walking. "Leonard?" you whisper. "Where are you? Leonard? Come back to me. The dead are walking. Where are you? Come back to me." This is not dementia. This is not hallucination. You have two years yet before your mind begins to slip. You have two years before you start to see Leonard and Gertie and pretty little children you don't know and flowers growing straight out of the carpet. You have two years before your memory comes unspooled. You will be embarrassed when you tell your niece tomorrow that you thought the mine rescue was the advent of the end times, that you called out for your long-dead husband, that you sat in the dark more thrilled than afraid. You don't know why Leonard doesn't come for you. You keep saying his name. You are not a religious zealot. You are not a crazy person. It is simply the fact that after all these years, after everything you've seen, you know that almost anything is possible. "Leonard," you say. "Please come back for me."

I Am the Voice Calling in the Desert

Truth be told, I love stained glass. My current church has great, arching, magnificent stained-glass windows in the sanctuary. They are nineteenth-century Methodist windows full of purples, golds, reds, and blues. Rich colors that drench sunlight. My church looks like a church: gray stone, wide front steps, wooden doors, a spire and a steeple. I do not understand these contemporary congregations who gather in glorified pole-barns. Miles of aluminum siding slapped up in a convenient location just off a highway. Certainly no stained glass. Those churches baffle me. Religion, now more than ever, needs at least a touch of majesty. And if church windows, the kind I'm talking about, are a thing of the past, where are we? Years ago, long before I was the pastor here, vandals broke one of our sanctuary windows, the southernmost window on the east side of the church. People talk of that act of vandalism so often, you'd think it happened yesterday. In my first year here, I found the broken panes of glass stacked behind the boiler in the basement. I had a couple of three-foot sections of the window restored and reframed, and I hung them in my office windows. My office, because it's down the classroom wing, has leaded glass instead of stained, and I appreciated the burst of color. But the congregation appreciated the act of restoration. There is nothing quite so satisfying as salvaging something that seemed lost.

I learned the importance of windows from my mother. A cardinal rule of my childhood was *thou shalt not touch windows*. Streaky, girl-sized fingerprints on glass were a ghastly offense in our house. At school, I once saw a child mash his face against a window and blow his cheeks out like a puffer fish. I nearly had a heart attack. I was sure the boy would be expelled or suspended, or at least paddled by the principal, if nothing else.

"Windows matter, Helen, believe me," my mother used to say. "Dirty windows indicate either carelessness or slothfulness. Both, as far as I'm concerned, are sins."

My earliest memory is of my mother washing windows. She wore pants for window washing, and a bandana tied around her hair. She removed all of the storm windows and lined them up along the fence in our backyard. It was my job to stand behind her holding out sheets of newspaper for drying the glass. When the storms were clean, my mother washed the permanent windows, first the outsides, which she reached with an extension ladder, and then the insides. It took us all day to do the windows, and by evening our house seemed transformed and alarmingly transparent. On the day we washed windows, my mother sent the curtains to the cleaner's. On any other evening, she would have drawn the drapes at sunset, but on window washing evenings, our lives were laid bare to the world through sparkling clear panes of glass. This one night of naked, open windows seemed my mother's proof. You see, those windows said, we have done as we should. Have a look. We haven't anything to hide.

"Windows," my mother once said, "are not just about us seeing out, Helen. They're about what others see when they look in. Think of that."

Then what of my love for stained glass? I'm not sure. It is a different sort of seeing that we're shooting for, I suppose. Something more metaphorical. Something more beautiful than even our very cleanest and best lives. I guess that's what we're trying to accomplish when we put up stained glass between ourselves and God.

This morning the sun is falling brilliantly through my office windows, so perhaps that is why I've been thinking of them. I spend a great deal of my time here—thinking, reading, preparing sermons—which makes me easy to find. I've lined the bookshelves with both sacred and secular texts, and I'm as likely to be reading a biography of Thomas Jefferson or a little Aristotle as I am to be reading anything from the mainline Christian presses. If God is worth His salt, He's more complicated and unknowable than any theologian's theory. And I hope He has a better sense of humor. Each new catalogue of books and videos from Focus on the Family that turns up in my mailbox makes me sigh and think, Well, Helen, all might be lost after all. But then I recycle the catalogue and soldier on.

And it is probably because I am thinking about windows and my mother and religion and politics that I don't hear Lindsay when she knocks at my office door. I am up on a chair, reaching to dust the very top shelf of my bookcase, completely oblivious to the timid rapping at my door, when Lindsay finally steps into the room and says, "Pastor?"

Someone who is less afraid than I am—this is what most people want in a pastor, and by and large, I can give that. I am usually more solid and dignified than I am in this particular moment, poised to climb onto the arm of my leather chair. I am a bit pear-shaped for climbing on chairs. When I turn around, one leg hoisted up in the air, Lindsay looks quite prepared to be mortified for me.

"Good heavens, Lindsay, hello," I say, and clamber

down.

"I knocked, but you didn't—"

"I know. I can get so totally swept away sometimes. I'm sorry. Please come in."

Lindsay is looking paler than usual, which is a feat for a woman with white-blond hair and translucent skin. Lindsay is the type of woman who must order complete wardrobes out of pricey catalogues each season—everything matches. Even now, in her sixth month of her second pregnancy, she looks as if she's stepped from the pages of a magazine. It must take her hours to look so breezy and carefree.

"I didn't mean to bother you," Lindsay says, still hesitating at my threshold.

"Nonsense. I was just keeping myself occupied." I toss my dust cloth onto my desk and wipe my hands on my pants. "Tea? Coffee? Can I get you anything?"

"No, thank you," Lindsay says.

"I might, if you don't mind."

"No, go ahead. Please."

I gesture Lindsay toward one of the leather armchairs. Instead of sitting, she stands beside the chair and examines the titles on my bookshelf. She smooths her hair with her thin fingers. I pour hot water from my electric teapot over a teabag. I am mentally running through a list of reasons for Lindsay's visit. I have been a pastor for many years now, and I know the human compulsion toward confession is powerful. I believe I could hear almost anything without a flicker of surprise. I stir sugar into my tea and then lean against my desk, since Lindsay doesn't seem inclined to sit.

"It's a lovely day, isn't it?" I ask.

"Yes. Fall has always been my favorite."

"Mmmmm," I say.

"And now with Dustin in kindergarten, for a few

months I've got the house to myself."

"What a treat," I say.

"Especially since I know it will only be until December. It's nice for a change—so quiet—but I think I'd go crazy if it were just me, all alone in that big house everyday. Crazy, I really think. It's quite a relief when Dustin comes home in the afternoons."

"I can imagine," I say.

"Of course it would be different if I were used to it. I'm sure living alone would be wonderful if I weren't so accustomed to Ted and Dustin. I didn't mean it had to be lonely."

"I didn't think you did," I say, and smile.

People often assume I am lonely. And by people, I mean women. They pity my childlessness even more than my husbandlessness. Back when I turned the corner into my forties, I noticed a shift in the way women treated me. A dogged hopefulness edged into resignation and sympathy. From my observations, however, rearing children is often an ignoble and undignified struggle. I am most often relieved when the last of my congregation's children have been strapped into minivans and SUVs and trucked home on Sundays. Children are so rarely as one would hope them to be.

Perhaps I know this better than most women because my mother never quite recovered from the disappointment of me. My mother, with her smart, A-line skirts and her curlers and her kitchen that always smelled of bleached flour and coffee and citrus had dreams for me that I ruined. Who wouldn't want a pretty daughter, the kind whose soft, natural curls are always tugging free of ribbons and ponytails? The kind who will live just piously enough to marry un-ironically in a gorgeous white dress, the whole church beaming as she floats down the aisle? It is not my mother's fault that that's what she wanted, or that she was more or less undone when she got me.

"It's Dustin, really, that I've come to talk to you about," Lindsay says.

"Ah, Dustin," I say. "Any particular trouble?"

"Oh, we're not having trouble with Dustin. I mean, not exactly. He's very well behaved and he's ahead of his peer group in kindergarten. He's fine that way. It's just, there's a small situation that's come up, and I told Ted I'd come see you about it."

"I'm happy to listen," I say. "Please sit. Make yourself comfortable."

"This is embarrassing," Lindsay says, perching on the very edge of a chair. "You're going to think I've lost my wits, Helen."

"I doubt it," I say.

"Dustin doesn't seem to understand prayer," Lindsay says. "He's rather confused about what it's for."

"How so?"

"The other day he told me he'd prayed that God would bless the toothpaste. He wanted to see a miracle, so he prayed that God would prevent the toothpaste from running out."

"I see."

"And he thinks it's working, Helen. That's the worst part. He's positive the toothpaste should have run out by now. You should see him. He's beside himself with glee."

I know I shouldn't, but I laugh. I can just picture the child, as pleased with himself as a Cheshire cat. Without warning, Lindsay bursts into tears.

"We've tried to teach him who God is and how to pray, and this is what we get for it. A fantasy about blessed toothpaste! It's not normal!"

Which is what this is all about, anyway. Parents want from their pastors what they want from their pediatricians—

an absolute assurance that their child is both normal and exceptional. It's a bit much to ask.

"Please, Lindsay," I say. "I'm sorry, dear. I didn't mean to laugh. There's no need to cry, really. This is not that big of a deal."

I hand Lindsay a box of Puffs, and she pulls out several tissues. Some counselors would suggest that it's unwise to ever diminish the significance of a person's fears, but in the practical world of getting through one day after the next, it's essential to delineate between those things that are and are not big deals. World hunger, natural disaster, the AIDS epidemic, teen pregnancy, homelessness, war—these are legitimate big deals. It would be nice if we, as the Body of Christ, could get our act in gear on these issues. But at the moment I have a distraught mother in my office pulling tissue after tissue out of a box of Puffs, and it's toothpaste that's upsetting her.

"I just feel like Ted and I are failing Dustin spiritually, and he isn't even in first grade."

"Oh," I say, waving a hand, "many children imagine a direct experience of the divine. It's a natural part of growing up. Dustin's just exploring, that's all."

Lindsay considers this for a long moment before asking, "But what happens when the toothpaste runs out?"

I can see the wheels turning in her head, the plans evolving to devise a system for pumping toothpaste from a new tube into the tube Dustin believes blessed. The pumping will have to happen in the middle of the night, and now not only will Lindsay have to breathe life into the mystery of Santa Claus, the Easter Bunny, and the Tooth Fairy, she will be the keeper and perpetuator of blessed toothpaste as well. I can see how a mother's life can get very complicated.

"He'll probably have forgotten all about this blessed business by that time. And if not, it'll be a fine opportunity to talk with him about miracles in the Bible. Why God does what He does. Dustin's quite perceptive. He's not too young for any of that."

When I say this, I'm speaking mostly of Christ's miracles, his extravagant mercy. Who could argue the goodness of healing lepers or raising kind old Lazarus from the dead? We talk precious little about Christ's final miracle—healing the centurion's ear, the one his disciple cut off. Christ laying his healing hands on the wounded flesh even of his mortal enemy. I hope Lindsay will speak to Dustin of such things and leave be some of the standard Old Testament tales. Noah and his Ark show up in an overwhelming number of feel-good children's books and videos, but honestly, he makes me nervous. How many tales of global annihilation should the average toddler consume? There's a catchy tune about the battle of Jericho, but the actual story ends with every breathing inhabitant of the city—man, woman, child, chicken, goat—being put to the sword. Every breathing inhabitant, that is, except for Rahab the prostitute and her family. Perhaps Dustin is too young for Joshua and his battle for Jericho. I am of the mind that we haven't nearly enough cogent adult supervision when it comes to Bible stories.

For example, I remember with disturbing clarity the day I learned about John the Baptist in Sunday school. There was very little religion talk in my home growing up aside from the ubiquitous saying of grace before meals. But we were dutiful, church-going Methodists as far back as I can remember. My parents believed church was essential for developing character, and about once a month we got up early enough to make it to Sunday school before the service. My class got the John the Baptist story in one fell swoop in the hour before church—everything from John leaping in Elizabeth's belly, to his baptizing of the Christ, to his gory and romantic head-on-a-silver-platter demise. I despised the daughter of Herodias, that insipid dancing girl who tricked her stepfather king into executing John. She must have been a very evil, a very wicked little thing. I was only capable of skimming the surface, of arranging facts into a chronology and shouting breathlessly over lunch, "And then the king had John's head cut off and presented to the queen on a silver platter!!"

"Please, Helen," my mother said, "not at the table."

"We're right here," my father said. "There's no need to shout."

I was left to ruminate and puzzle about John the Baptist on my own. I read the verses from the Gospels that our teacher had printed on note cards for us to take home. Much of it was incomprehensible to me, but I took pleasure in the cadence of the language, if not the sense. I dragged all of my dolls out into the backyard and began preaching to them, pretending I was John the Baptist with a flock of followers. In my imagination, preaching required a great deal of running back and forth and waving my arms around. It was oddly akin to some sort of fit.

"Talk to Dustin," I say to Lindsay. "Try to understand what he's thinking."

"Oh, he's very sensitive," Lindsay says. "He is quite astute. Sometimes, when I'm worried, he's the one to remind me to pray. I really think I'm learning as much from him as he's learning from me about how to be."

"I can imagine," I say.

"That's why this all seems so important," she says. "I'm not sure you can really understand how terribly crucial it feels, to give him everything, to be sure he understands. We're the ones he'll hold responsible, after all."

"I suppose that's true."

"I mean, here we are in this terrible world, and we have to give him something to hold onto. We have to protect him and prepare him all at the same time. He's the center of our lives. They are, I guess. Dustin and his little sister."

Her hand travels over the globe of her belly. I'm struck by a look of fear that flashes in her eyes. How daunting to be a parent, to have to stand in the gap for a small child, to be directly responsible for propping up and affirming his faith, even if that means lying or withholding the truth. I ask myself, sometimes, if that's not what pastors do—smooth the path, oil the gears to cut down on resistance, make the great mysteries of life simpler, easier to swallow. I tell you, half the things we learn in seminary, most pastors spend their careers sidestepping. My life as a pastor would be far easier and more pleasant if God were the magician we imagine as children—kind and capricious—the blesser of toothpaste.

What Lindsay and I have not yet spoken of, however, is that this matter of the toothpaste is not just about whom God is and what God does. Dustin prayed for this miracle. Dustin, at the moment, has God at his bidding. Children are natural narcissists, astonished by their own existence, by how fortunate the world is to have them in its midst. The discovery that you are no more or less important than any other individual walking around on two legs is one of the great shocks of the human experience. It seems a shock from which many fail to recover. You would be surprised by the number of boys in congregations across America who fancy themselves the reincarnation of Christ. I have heard that some Catholic girls live in a similar ecstasy of fear concerning Immaculate Conception and virgin birth. My heavens, who wouldn't be terrified by such things?

We Protestants don't talk much about Mary, so I suppose we spare our girls that. Even had I been Catholic, I can't imagine my obsessions tending toward the Marian. It was John the Baptist who caught my imagination. I was an only child, so I felt a kindred connection with John's experience in the desert—his self-styled monasticism. I had romantic notions about wearing goatskins and letting my hair grow wild, eating only locusts and honey. Even now, I think it is possible to be so finely tuned to the Holy Spirit that you look a little untamed to the outside world. As a child I was taken by the idea of a borderland between sanctified and just plain crazy. John the Baptist baptized Christ—imagine that. He stormed through the deserts of first-century Palestine like a wildfire through prairie grass, clearing a path. Who wouldn't want to do that? My mother, for one, I suppose. She had her own opinions about the proper imaginary life of a young girl.

"So it's a girl," I say to Lindsay. If she has come to talk with me about Dustin, we have finished, but she has made no motion to leave.

"We haven't actually found out. It just seems there are so few genuine surprises left in life. So few wonderful surprises, that is. But Ted and I feel certain it's a girl. She feels like a girl in there."

"A girl would be nice."

"A girl worries me a little. I think boys must be easier."

"In what ways?" I ask.

"Oh, I don't know," Lindsay says. She stands and crosses to the window, peering around my framed chunk of stained glass out at the parking lot. "I don't know what I'm talking about. You have to worry your whole life about girls. They're never quite safe."

"Safe from what?"

"But boys aren't either, I guess. Ted says I'm just hormonal," Lindsay says. "He says it's a pregnancy thing. But I get this way sometimes, pregnant or not. I just don't always tell him about it."

"What way? What's troubling you, Lindsay?"

"Life." She turns from the window and pulls a volume of Bonhoeffer from my bookshelf. She thumbs through the first few pages and then sets the text on the window ledge. "I don't think life has been fair to me," she says. "I think it's been too good. I think everything I've ever wanted has fallen into place and I'm just holding my breath, waiting for whatever's coming that will balance things out."

"Like what?"

"Tragedy. Some disaster. You can't have everything all the time. It's like I've got a cup of water and someone keeps pouring more water into it. More and more and more and now the water is up to the very top. It's up over the top, actually. It's just surface tension holding everything in. Which is why I can't move. If I breathe wrong the water's going to spill over the lip. I keep hoping, praying, almost, for some small bad thing to happen. Something to take the pressure off. I feel like if some small bad thing doesn't happen soon, everything could fall apart."

"And what would that mean?" I ask.

"Ted. He could leave me. Or get hit by a bus, or something. Being Ted's wife is who I am. If he vanished, if he just disappeared into thin air, I'd be lost. I know that's not the sort of thing women are supposed to say anymore, but it's how I feel.

"Or Dustin. I try to imagine, sometimes, what I would do if he was kidnapped. I try to go through it, step by step, and imagine what I would feel. Or if he got cancer or got killed in a car accident. I'd go crazy. Really, Helen. I'm not the kind of woman who could rise above. I would descend into this terrible abyss and never surface again." Lindsay's cheeks are pink and she blinks rapidly, her mascaraed lashes beating back tears. She takes a deep breath and whatever emotion has threatened her seems to pass. "I try to think about this baby. If something happened to her, I mean now, while it's still a pregnancy and not quite a person, that would be better. That would be perfect, almost. A very large small-bad-thing. It would be terrible, but then Ted and Dustin would be safe. I feel like they'd be off-limits, somehow. Isn't that horrible? But if anyone gave me a choice, sacrifice this pregnancy and keep everything else just the way it is, forever, I'd do it."

Sometimes, even my pastor-self does not know what to say. Ted might leave Lindsay. Husbands do such things regularly. And something terrible could happen to Dustin. If not now, if not some catastrophe of childhood, who is to say that he won't fling himself down a path of drugs and destruction as a teenager? Nothing is impossible. But don't we all live on the brink of disaster? We all live our lives on a high wire. We just don't know it unless someone or something gives us a reason to look down. Perhaps Lindsay is right about children, though. Perhaps they are always and forever that reason to look down.

And the uncanny thing about children is the way their lives can go underground. There they are, living in the sphere of your existence, yet with complicated lives you have no access to. I wonder if we are that to God sometimes—perplexing little creatures who take what we are given, squirrel it away, and turn it into something completely different with our imaginations? I am suspicious of Lindsay's life arithmetic. Small things are sometimes not that small. And large things—terrible, looming, life-sized bad things—can be managed. My fascination with John the Baptist probably looked small, initially. Often we cannot judge the magnitude or scale of things until they are upon us.

"What on earth are you playing?" my mother asked one afternoon when she stepped out into the yard to hang up the wash. I was barefoot, streaked with dirt, and I'd torn my shirt.

"John the Baptist," I said.

I must have been quite an affront to my mother in that moment. It broke her heart that I could never manage to keep bobby socks from slipping down and getting sweaty and crumpled in my shoes, and here I was, looking for all the world like a mental patient.

"John the Baptist wasn't a girl," she said, reasonably. "If you set your dolls up on the patio you could play school."

I shrieked and ran around behind the garage where I could kick up dust and preach my sermons in peace.

"Don't come into my house dirty, Helen," my mother called after me. "Wash up at the hose and put on something clean before dinner."

That evening I arrived at the table as she'd asked, clean and in a fresh skirt and blouse, but my mother made her displeasure with me known over supper. She regaled my father with my outlandish behavior as she passed around the stewed beef and mashed potatoes.

"Would you please speak to her, Wallace?" she asked. "Helen is absolutely out of her wits."

"She's fine, Joyce," my father said. It was not uncommon for my parents to discuss me over dinner. I listened with excitement and curiosity—what would they make of me?! I turned my head as if I were at a tennis match. "The girl is fine. You're just encouraging her."

"No one's encouraging me," I piped up.

"Please be quiet, Helen," my father said, and we all ate our dinner in tranquility.

As my imaginary life took on more and more significance, my parents grew further and further away from me. It was as if I were in a fish tank and we were watching each other through the glass. They thought they could see all of me, but they couldn't.

I lived breathlessly in the backyard, baptizing everything I could get my hands on. I splashed furiously in buckets of water and went wild with the garden hose. I called endlessly for my dolls to repent. I made straight the path for the coming of the Lord. The wonderful and terrible thing about preparing for the Second Coming is that it brings with it the Day of Reckoning. I began spending more time than a child should thinking about hell. I looked at strangers in the supermarket with a deep sense of curiosity. Whose name would we find recorded in the Book of Life and who would be cast into the Lake of Fire? On the last day, we are told, all will be made known. Judgment is thrilling but also enough to chill you to the marrow. I began to fear for my parents. I called to them, but they could not hear. One evening, as I played long into the gathering dusk in the backyard, my mother stood in the open door of the laundry porch, framed in light from the kitchen behind her, calling my name. The sight of her pulled me out of what must have looked like a snarling rant of gibberish. I was holding a soaking wet Barbie doll in each fist.

"Mama," I said.

"Come here, Helen," my mother said.

She sat on the stoop and held her arms out to me. I went to her like someone in a trance, those outstretched mother's arms calling to me. She hugged me and pulled me onto her lap. She pushed my matted head against her breast.

"Helen," my mother said, and I could hear the way her voice echoed in her hollow chest, "what's happening to you?"

"It's the end of the age, Mama," I said.

Her arms went slack around me. Her dress smelled like laundry soap. Her skin smelled of powder and of makeup—wax and animal fat.

"What age, Helen?"

"He comes like a thief in the night," I said. I could

feel hot tears in my eyes, and I knew how they would look, cutting a pink path through the dirt on my face.

"You need a bath," my mother said. I tried to slip free of her as she stood, but she hefted me into her arms. She was still strong enough to pick me up if she had to.

"No," I howled, struggling.

"Helen, stop it," she said, her arms like a vice around me. I kicked and screamed and twisted. "Wallace!" my mother shouted. "Please fill the tub. Helen needs a bath."

My father leapt from his chair in the living room when he saw us. He reached out to take me from my mother's arms, but she turned us away from him.

"I have her, Wallace," she said. "Please draw a bath. The girl is filthy."

In my memory, I fought her valiantly as she struggled me upstairs, stripped me naked, and plopped me into the steaming water my father had readied in the tub. I think, though, I probably flailed and sobbed pathetically. We are rarely as heroic or strong as we fancy ourselves to be. My mother didn't cry or shout or argue. She held my arm firmly in her right hand and a bar of soap in her left. She scrubbed and splashed until I was clean and so worn out that I sat meekly in the gray, cooling water and let her wash my hair. She was nearly as wet as me by the time she helped me out of the tub and rubbed me down with a towel.

"You have to snap out of this, Helen," she said as she dried me. "You have to pull yourself together. You're acting like a baby with this ridiculous business, and I won't have it anymore."

She shook me by the shoulders when I wouldn't look at her. She thought I was being sullen, but I was actually mourning the great gulf that had opened between us, our inability to reach each other across such a perilous divided. How could I feel otherwise when I thought she might soon be lost to me forever? I could imagine her, cowering and small, being cast into the Lake of Fire.

"Do you hear me, Helen?" she asked, holding my wet head in both of her hands.

"Yes," I said.

"Good. Now go to bed."

I could feel her eyes on me as I walked out of the bathroom and down the hall toward my room, the carpet soft and springy under my bare, wrinkled feet.

"Do you think it's possible to keep things as they are now, forever?" I ask Lindsay.

"Of course not," she says. "I'm not a fool. I'm just talking, thinking out loud, really."

"I don't think you're a fool," I say.

Lindsay smiles, unkindly. She and I are not friends. I am a professional listener. She's my congregant. That is the extent of our relationship. Pastoring can be lonely work for that reason.

"No, I know, Helen, forgive me," she says. So many small requests for forgiveness a person must send up every day. "Ted's right. I think I am hormonal. I've been snipping at everyone just like that lately. Aren't I terrible?"

"No, dear," I say. "You're not. Have a seat. Let me make you a cup of tea. Really, you're welcome here."

Lindsay crosses back to my leather chair. She drops heavily onto her seat and pulls her hair free from its ponytail. She shakes her head and runs her fingers through her loose hair. I turn the teakettle back up to high, and when it whistles, I pour the water into Lindsay's cup. Lindsay holds the cup in her hands, close to her face, blowing on the water as the tea steeps.

"You wouldn't tell anyone, would you?" she asks, after we have sat together quietly for several minutes.

"What?"

"About what I said. About the baby. Being willing

to sacrifice it. It makes me sick to even say it again. I didn't mean that, really, you know."

"Of course," I say. "Of course you didn't. And I don't share personal conversations. Not with anyone."

Lindsay tips her head. Her find blond hair falls white and gold around her face for a moment before she sweeps it back into a ponytail again with two or three efficient strokes of her hands. "I've been bothered by a recurring dream lately," she says. "Maybe that's what's got me so out of sorts. I hardly ever remember my dreams, but this one has really been getting to me. I dream it two, three times a week."

"What is it?"

"It's just a pregnancy dream. But it's creepy. In the dream I have the baby, but instead of skin, the baby has scales. And a mouth full of sharp little teeth. Isn't that absurd? I'm beside myself, of course, but I try to hide that there's anything wrong from Ted. I keep thinking that if I can only love this little lizard-baby enough, Ted will see that it's fine and won't leave me. I try to feed it, but its teeth—"

"That's frightening."

"It's like something from a lousy alien movie. It's not even original."

"But still," I say.

"Yes, still. It keeps me up. I've been losing sleep."

We ask our dreams to reveal things. The Pharaoh asked Joseph to interpret his dreams. Seven fat cows consumed by seven thin. The angel Gabriel came to Mary in a dream. John's Revelation was revealed through spinning, waking dreams. *Your young men will see visions, your old men will dream dreams.* How strange and terrifying our own minds can be. I am suspicious of mysticism. Our imaginations are capable of most anything, and for that reason I'm disinclined to let the imagination have sway over religion. But when I was a child, I reasoned like a child, and I let my fantasy life run wild. I believed religion to be something it turned out not to be.

I don't know what would have become of my obsession with John the Baptist if not for that dream. A few weeks after my bathtub struggle with my mother, I dreamed our church was falling down. I was sitting in the pew between my mother and father, when we were all overpowered by an oppressive heat. I felt as if I were swimming in steam. The pastor was preaching in the pulpit, but I couldn't hear him. His mouth moved but he might as well have been speaking under water. I tried to say something to my mom or my dad, but I discovered that they were asleep and that I couldn't speak. All around me, members of the congregation were falling dead asleep, sliding out of the pews, dropping into the aisles, slumping over onto the people in front of them. I wanted to shout "Wake up! Wake up!" but I could hardly open my mouth. Soon the whole sanctuary began to shake, from the foundation to the rafters. The chandeliers swung dangerously and the plaster in the ceiling split. Drywall dust rained down on us. The walls crumbled in, great chunks of brick and mortar tumbling down around me, and I tried again to shout, but by this point I could not breathe.

I woke alone in my bedroom in a cold sweat. The house was quiet save for the muffled sound of my father snoring down the hall. The streetlamp outside my window made it impossible to tell the time of night. I felt changed by my dream. I felt spoken to. I felt singled out. That night, I lay in my cold bed, teeth chattering, trying to divine what action God wanted me to take. By morning I had a plan that thrilled and frightened me. My plan, thinking back on it now, was quite silly, but it did not seem silly to me then. Nor was it silly to my mother. It proved once and for all that I was not and would never be, and in fact certainly haven't been, the daughter she had hoped for. Even now, when I go to visit her, my wisp of a mother roaming a world of dementia to which I have no access, she speaks of it often. I sit by her bed and stroke her thin hair. I hold her bony hand, and she tells me about what a wicked child she had, what a naughty little girl. Sometimes she tells me her daughter died years ago. On other days, she looks at me in a moment of shocking recognition and says, "Oh, Helen, where have you been?"

I dreamed my dream on a Friday night and my plan was for Sunday morning, which left only one long, nervous Saturday to get through. By evening, I was an anxious wreck.

"Are you feeling all right, Helen?" my mother asked that evening when I came into the kitchen for dinner. "You look pale. Are you ill?"

"I'm fine," I said.

She lay her palm against my forehead and said, cautiously, "You don't feel hot."

"Because I'm not sick."

"Don't snap, Helen," she said. "It's impolite." She wiped her hands on her apron and poured me a glass of milk.

On Saturday evenings, I was given something simple for dinner, like a grilled cheese and tomato sandwich in the kitchen, while my mother ironed dress clothes for the service in the morning out on the laundry porch. Later that night, she and my father would have a nice dinner alone together in the dining room. I never resented them that. In fact, I loved Saturday nights. They are some of my fondest memories from childhood. The wall between us was good for my mother and me. We chatted through the open door between the kitchen and the porch, and sometimes she told me stories that she otherwise wouldn't have—stories about going to dances with my father, or about the clubs she and her friends were in during high school. I loved the sound of the water sloshing in the iron and then the puff and sigh of steam. I loved the faint but particular smell of spray starch on damp cloth. On that Saturday, however, I said little. I tore my sandwich into tiny pieces but could eat very little of it. When I said I was finished my mother considered the scraps of sandwich on my plate for a moment but didn't make me eat any more.

"Run on to bed, Helen," she said. "I'll see you in the morning, dear."

"Goodnight, Mom," I said.

In the morning, we reached the church just as the organist broke into the processional. My father shepherded my mother and me into a pew off the center aisle. The choir entered first, followed closely by the acolytes and the pastor. We had no girl acolytes then as most churches do now, and I envied those boys in their small robes cinched up with gold cords. I would have lit the candles magnificently if anyone had let me. The boys tended to jostle each other and rarely managed to light their candles in unison. Some of them were rather large and fat for their age and looked ridiculous stuffed into too-short robes with their sneakers showing. But by that morning, my fantasies had reached much further than being an acolyte. I saw clearly that those acolytes were just boys, mere children.

I sat closest to the aisle, my mother on my right, and my father just beyond her. This seemed satisfactory since I knew I would have to evade my parents' grasping hands when I stood up to do what I had to do. Just the thought of it made me dizzy. My mother was quicker to reach out and pull me in when I stepped out of line in any way, but my father's arms were longer than hers. If I moved quickly, in two steps I could be out of my mother's reach. I managed to get through all of the opening hymns that morning, although my heart was racing and I felt at one point I might faint with all the standing up and sitting down and searching for page numbers in the dusty hymnal. After the singing was over, I refused to go to the front of the sanctuary for the children's message.

"Helen, honey, that's you," my mother said when the pastor invited the kids down to the altar and I didn't move.

I sat stone still, even when my mother slipped a hand behind my lower back and tried to use her arm as a lever to lift me out of the pew.

"What's the matter with you?" she asked.

"I'm not a child today," I said.

"Good grief," my mother said.

"Hush, both of you," my father whispered. "If Helen doesn't want to go up for the children's message, she'll just miss out."

My mother said something more, but for the life of me, I've never been able to remember what it was. The pastor's brief children's message concluded, and all of the children who'd been tossed up at the altar drew back into the pews with their parents, as if caught in a receding tide. I recognized my moment when the pastor stepped up to the pulpit and paused. I believed I'd had a vision and that the silence of my dream would be broken when I opened my mouth and let the voice of the Holy Spirit pour out.

"Hark!" I shouted and leapt from the pew a split-second too fast for my mother to stop me. Hark was the most Biblical word I could come up with.

"Helen!" my mother and father said in unison. The congregation stirred and turned and murmured, and Pastor Whalen looked up from his notes.

"I've had a vision from God, Pastor Whalen," I said.

I could feel my parents leaving their pew in pursuit of me, but the pastor raised one hand and stopped them.

"Yes, Helen?" he said.

I could see in his face that he was laughing at me. He didn't smile, but it was there in the lift of his eyebrows and the curious angle at which he held his head. He was humoring a child, but I forged ahead.

"The judgment of the Lord is upon us," I said, and to this very day I can remember the way it felt to speak, as if the words were a river flowing through me, not a series of sounds my throat and tongue and lungs chose to make. "I've seen each and every one of you fall asleep. I've felt the earth quake with God's anger, and if you don't repent, God will bury you alive under the stones of this very church!"

The bit about being buried alive was shocking, even for me. My mother and father looked at me as if we had never met. Pastor Whalen smiled and then laughed.

"God says you, too," I said, looking him straight in the face.

Most everyone in the pews looked down at their bulletins, which had been typed up and copied on a Ditto machine the previous evening by Pastor Whalen's wife, as if searching for some way to account for this outburst in the orderly plan for the service. I didn't know what to do after delivering my message from God, so I fell down on the floor. I thought it would have been far more appropriate if I'd lost consciousness, but I never did. I just lay quietly on the soft, brown carpet of the church floor for what seemed like many minutes before my father collected himself enough to apologize loudly, hoist me into a fireman's carry over his shoulder, and direct my mother to please follow him. I looked up as I was being lugged out of the sanctuary and shouted, "God has spoken!" before my mother clapped her hand over my mouth. My father spanked me soundly in the parking lot, which was embarrassing for a child of my age, but all in all I felt the whole thing had gone well.

"Are you out of your mind, Helen?" my mother asked once we were all buckled into the car. She turned in her seat to look at me, and I was astonished to see her eyes welling up with tears. "Are you hell-bent on humiliating your father and me?"

I looked out the window because it made me too sad to look at my mother, her pretty face growing blotchy as she fought her desire to cry.

"What I really think, though," Lindsay says, "is that all of this is bigger than just how I feel about my family."

"What do you mean?" I ask. Isn't everything, always, somehow, about our family? Aren't we all tied together, for better or for worse, like great lumbering fools in a three-legged race?

"I mean the world," Lindsay says. The world. There is that. "It's so unstable, now, isn't it? It just seems that at any moment everything could come unhinged."

"I know," I say. "I think it could."

Lindsay looks at me as if I've gone off script. I try to smile. I shrug.

"Do you think it's the end times?" she asks. "I'd never really thought about the end times before, but I've been listening to what they're saying on the radio. On the Christian station. They say it's all in Revelations. What do you think?"

"I think most of the time, those of us who do the talking, don't have any idea what we're talking about."

"That's not the most comforting thing I've heard a pastor say," Lindsay says.

"I know."

Back in seminary, I often told the story of condemning my childhood church. It was always good for a laugh. My soon-to-be pastor friends and I could best appreciate the story because it rang true for almost everyone, the need to curb and harness a zeal that threatened to run roughshod over us.

We could laugh at me, but also, and more gently perhaps, at poor Pastor Whalen, having to do something with this shouting child in his sanctuary. In seminary, we could see ourselves from both ends.

Later, after a number of years as a pastor, I shared with some friends the first half of the aftermath of my outcry. We were having dinner together at a nice restaurant, celebrating one among us who had been transferred to a ministry in a distant city. We were talking about the path we had chosen, about our churches, about our lives. The pastor who was leaving us mentioned that he had never quite gotten a handle on his congregation's bent toward judgment. His congregation had long been more fire-and-brimstone than he was. The rest of us nodded, sipped wine, chewed French bread.

"The thing about judgment is this—it is almost always a disappointment," I said.

"True, true," the only other lady pastor among us said.

I told of how patiently I waited for God's judgment to fall on our congregation and about how it never did. I told of how I felt like a modern-day Jonah of Nineveh, how I wanted to languish under a palm tree, but as we only had some juniper bushes out back, I languished under those. I made a parody of myself, this wistful child waiting for judgment to rain down from the sky while her mother eyeballed her relentlessly and her father pretended that nothing whatsoever had happened.

"Perhaps, Helen," a friend said, the lip of his wine glass resting thoughtfully against his chin, "the congregation was sinning very quietly and privately, as we've all come to know that people do, and at your warning, they quit." He raised his eyebrows and tipped his glass to his lips.

"How satisfying is that?" I asked, and we all laughed. "That's what I'm saying. Any way you slice it, judgment disappoints. And if God chose to rain fire from heaven, I'd bet you anything that we'd all be Lot's wife, pillars of salt. How many of us could stand it, not turning around to watch?"

What I did not tell my friends around the dinner table, and what I have never told anyone before or since, is what happened when Pastor Whalen came over to talk some sense into me. He came on a Saturday afternoon. Once he was comfortably seated in the living room, one ankle propped on his opposite knee, I was summoned from the backyard to apologize. I stood in the doorway leaning against my mother's shoving hands like a stubborn mule.

"Helen," Pastor Whalen said patiently. He sighed and smiled and turned his eyes first toward the ceiling and then toward me. "I think it would be a good idea if we talked. Come on in, Helen. Don't be afraid. I'm not angry with you."

"Apologize to the pastor, Helen," my mother said.

"I'm not sorry," I said. "I was given a message from God."

"God is not in the habit of making prophets out of little girls," Pastor Whalen said. "Could you give us a moment, Joyce?" he asked.

"Of course," my mother said, and melted from the room. She was more than happy to turn me over to our pastor. I can't say I blame her. I had long since ceased to be a child that she could comprehend.

"I think you might be getting just a little too big for your britches, don't you?" Pastor Whalen asked.

"'And it shall come to pass in the last days, saith God, I will pour out my Spirit upon all flesh; and your sons and your daughters shall prophesy, and your young men shall see visions and your old men shall dream dreams,'" I quoted from the book of Acts. "I'm one of those daughters, Pastor Whalen," I said. "It says at the end of the age we will prophesy, right there in the Bible. You can't stand in my way."

"Ah," he said, "so we're quoting Scripture, I see. You might find the letters of Paul even more illuminating. Try First Corinthians. 'Let your women keep silence in the churches; for it is not permitted unto them to speak, but they are commanded to be under obedience, as also saith the law. And if they will learn anything, let them ask their husbands at home; for it is a shame for women to speak in the church.'"

It is difficult for a lady pastor to sidestep Paul in many denominations and congregations, even today. I am sure you can imagine how it might feel for a young girl to have 1 Corinthians laid at her feet in 1963. I had never thought to care about what Paul had to say about women. I'd only wanted the mystery and adventure of the apostles. I'd wanted to hear God calling my name.

"Are you listening to me, Helen?" Pastor Whalen asked, taking my slim shoulders firmly in his hands. "You've embarrassed your parents and yourself quite enough, don't you think? You're on the verge of becoming a very naughty little girl."

I have no witness for what happened next, and even I, in my most solid and sober moments, believe I was child plagued by her imagination. I was living in a fantasy world of my own making. I know that, but it does not change the fact that Pastor Whalen smiled at me, and his hands suddenly felt cold and hard on my arms. When I would not speak, or smile, or turn my eyes from his face, he licked his lips, and the tip of his tongue was forked like that of a snake. I saw his snake-tongue flick out at me twice, and then disappear between his lips. I know that I screamed and screamed with such hysteria that both my parents came bolting into the room. They found me struggling in the grip of an astonished Pastor Whalen, who kept repeating my name over and over as if I'd forgotten who I was. He turned me loose, and if he tried to explain anything to my parents, I could not hear him over my own screams. I threw myself at my father, and he pinned my arms between his chest and mine so I could not flail against him.

"It's okay, Helen," he said.

I could feel my mother's warm hands rubbing and thumping my back.

"What happened, honey? What's wrong?" she asked.

I just shook my head and buried my face against my father's shirt. When he kept on holding me, when he didn't put me down or scold me or turn me loose, I began to sob. My mother wrapped her arms around both of us. Later, this would all drive a wedge between us, but in my moment of fear, my mother helped my father hold me.

Lindsay pats her purse and her pockets in that way that has little to do with actually looking for anything and more to do with telegraphing one's intention to go.

"Thank you for all your help, Helen," she says. "You really are wonderful. I feel so much better about Dustin and everything."

"You're welcome," I say. "I'm always happy to see you. Stop in any time."

"I'm sorry to have interrupted," she says, waving a hand at my dust rag.

"Nonsense," I say. "Enjoy the day."

"It really is lovely out. Just perfect."

She does not say, See you Sunday, Pastor.

"I'll be seeing you, Lindsay," I say.

Her heels click on the hardwood of the hall, and then she is gone. I lift the dust rag from my desk. It has dried, of course, so I spray it again with Pledge. I move one of my nice chairs over a few feet so I can reach the next bookshelf. Perhaps I'm failing as a pastor. I don't know.

There are some things I have learned to say to no one. After whatever it was that happened in the living room with Pastor Whalen, I became a quiet child and endeavored diligently to be as normal as possible. I practiced being only as pious as the average American girl might be expected to be. Even to this day, sometimes when I blink, I can feel the chill of Pastor Whalen's hands on my skin and see the frightful, forked tongue slipping back behind his lips. But these are my own matters to puzzle out. If I had said a word about any of this during seminary, I probably would have been dismissed. It's just the sort of thing that the psychologists and counselors now employed to vet prospective members of the cloth might be on the lookout for. I have learned to pastor calmly, to keep to myself those things that might be tinged by visions or hysteria. I believe I have made a clean break from my delusions of the past, but every now and again I have a curious dream. It is a dream within a dream. In the dream, I am outside of my own body, watching myself sleep. The room suddenly resounds with the voice of John the Baptist crying: "I am the voice calling out in the desert!" I see myself wake with a start. I see myself freeze with panic as John's voice echoes and then fades. And then I realize I am still watching myself from a distance—I am still dreaming—so I must wake again and lie with the blood rushing in my ears until my eyes adjust to the dark.

Wake in the Night

Wake in an upstairs bedroom of an old farmhouse in the middle of the night. The west-facing window gapes open. The night breathes. Curtains lift and stir. Somewhere, a hundred-year-old joist creaks. Blink. The night is dark. How much can you see? The night is so quiet you can hear your own blood rushing through your circulatory system. You can feel your pulse in the hollow of your throat. Your skin prickles with a light sweat. Breathe.

Stretch your arms and your legs and slip out from under the thin sheet. Feel the fine grit of the floorboards beneath your feet. You are naked and your limbs feel strong. Pull on a pair of gym shorts and a t-shirt. Your sneakers are waiting at the foot of the bed. Lace them up. Tie a double knot. You are getting out of here. Are you frightened? Does your blood thin with adrenaline?

Take the stairs. The banister is smooth in the way wood is smoothed by a century of human hands. The stairs complain with your weight. After each step you listen but no one stirs. No one seems to be there. You haven't turned on any lights so you descend the stairs in darkness. The stairs lead into the kitchen. A butcher's block runs through the center of the large room, as old as the house it's in, its surface scored. There is a zinc sink and counter beneath the southern window. There are no cupboards, just open shelves stacked with dishes and canisters and little jars of spices and a whole wall of shelves lined with canning jars, their contents mysterious in this light. Through the window over the sink you can see Scorpio climbing in the southern sky. Lock the window you came in through.

Throw the back door and you are suddenly out of the silence of the strange house and into the night. Leave the door standing open. A tree frog, its suckered feet sticking it to a window, sings for a mate. The stars wheel in slow motion above you, pinioned by Polaris. From the back porch you can see black fields stretching away to the tree line—a ragged border of starless black at the horizon—marking a river in the distance. Coyotes yip. To the west and the east you can see the glow of dusk-to-dawns on other farms. The Milky Way is a river of hazy light cutting a swath above you. Does the sky make you dizzy? A little seasick?

Find a bicycle in the garage. An old ten-speed, what was once called a boy's bike. The frame is dusty and the brakes squeak but the tires are firm and the chain has been oiled. Someone must have ridden it recently, or, perhaps, simply prepared it for you. A cat meows at you from the garage rafters. Something else scuttles in the woodpile. Mount the bike. The tires click. Snug your sneakered toes into the clips. Pedal down the drive under two aging silver oaks, their dead branches like threatening fingers protruding beyond their leafy ones. Once out on the road and gaining speed, click up into a higher gear and then ride down in the drops, the handlebar tape sticky against your palms, your fingers ready to reach for the brakes. The tires hum against tarmac. Weeds whip past in the ditch. Pedal faster until your thighs burn and your chest aches and then coast. You are pedaling east, toward morning, toward a day that hasn't happened yet.

About a half a mile in front you, there is a dark house set back in the middle of a field. The hay has recently been mown and furrowed into rows to dry before it is baled. The hay is so sweetly fragrant it almost stinks. As you approach you see the house is certainly abandoned, no drive cuts through the field, no telephone or electrical wires

tether the house to the lines that run parallel to the road. Grip your brakes. Slip your right foot from the toe clip as you slow to a stop. Lightning bugs flicker in the field. The road is empty, the house you woke in far behind you. A toad hops out of the weeds and thumps against your shin. You cry out and jerk backwards, almost toppling over the bike between your legs. The toad takes two panicked hops and then freezes in the middle of the road. Perhaps hoping stillness makes it invisible. Your heart hammers. You want to laugh.

Why do you leave the bike in the ditch and set out across the field toward the house? The stubble of the mown hay is sharp and brittle. Distressed crickets and grasshoppers fling themselves in front of you. You think you see a small black snake. The hay field feels alive with insects and rodents and other life. A barred owl calls in the distance. You reach the listing front porch of the abandoned house. The floorboards are busted but the railing is filigreed with delicate gable. The windows, six feet from sill to sash, are boarded up on the first floor but gape open on the second— the emptiness of eyes put out. Step up onto the porch. The door has not been nailed shut with plywood. Try the knob. It rattles, loose in your hand, but the door is locked. Lift the brick sitting on the sill of the boarded-up window just to the left of the door. White larvae of something squirm on its underside. Beneath the brick is a skeleton key. You are a detective. You are on a mission. The key fits loosely into the keyhole of the front door. Feel the old bolt catch and slide back. The door swings open on rusty hinges. The house is pitch black and smells of dust and old grain and mouse droppings and you don't know what else. You would not dare set one foot inside this house if it weren't for the heavy-duty Maglite sitting just inside the doorframe. Lift the flashlight. Find the soft rubber of its switch and click it on. A shaft of light leaps through the darkness and the wall opposite you is suddenly illuminated. Peeling wallpaper. Wainscoting. Sacks of seed stacked up all the way down the hall. There is an old wall-mounted telephone at the end of the hall, its receiver dangling from the stretched-out coils of its cord.

Pull the door closed behind you. There are two arched doorways on either side of you, a staircase up to the second floor, slightly to your left, and then the hall that leads toward the back of the house. You sweep your flashlight through the two main rooms of the first floor. Each is now a storeroom: canisters of kerosene and gasoline and motor oil and spare mechanical parts. Beneath the dust and dirt and grime, the floorboards are parqueted. At the end of the hall you discover the kitchen. There is black and white checkerboard linoleum. An aluminum and Formica table in the middle of the room. Someone has left a pair of work gloves on the counter. A five-gallon water cooler sits in one corner. Behind the kitchen is a cement-floored lean-to. A mudroom. A cool place for milk or butter in the summer.

The front door of the house creaks open. Click off the flashlight. Freeze. Hold your breath. Your heart threatens you from the inside. You wonder if it is possible that this is a dream from which you will wake. Whoever has just opened the door fiddles with the knob. You have the key in your pocket. You left the brick turned up on the windowsill. "Someone here?" a voice asks. Battle your lungs. Refuse your ragged breath. Boots enter the hall. Then take the steps. When you hear feet on the landing above you, dash down the hall and out the door. Run blindly across the field. Grab the bike from the ditch and take off, toe clips hanging down under your feet. Pump the pedals until your heart hammers from physical exertion rather than from fright. Pedal until the abandoned house and the mown hayfield have vanished behind you. After a couple of miles turn right at an unmarked crossroad just before the fields give way to a stand of woods. A quarter moon has risen. Scorpio has climbed off toward the west. The moonlight casts your shadow into the ditch. The night reels around you.

When the road Ts, turn left. You are at the top of a steep hill, turning into the woods you have been skirting, but you would rather turn east, into the canopy, than head back west. Stop pedaling at the top of the hill. The bike carries you over, tipping toward the river basin beneath you, picking up speed and kicking gravel. Grip the handlebars. The bike jounces through a pothole, the tires skid on the gravel, the machine beneath you shudders and gives, but then rights itself, hurtling, speed keeping you upright. Hold on. Keep your eyes open. There is a green steel bridge over the river at the bottom of the hill. If you make it across the bridge you will coast to a stop in the river flats just to catch your breath. You hit the bridge. The decking is steel grating rather than a solid surface and the tires of the bike sing. You feel shot through with electricity. Above the tires and your heart and the wind in your face you hear girls shriek.

The tires go quiet when you hit the smooth, solid road and you coast. There is a car pulled way off to the side of the road, an old Buick Skylark. You come to a stop. The car is empty. The voices of the girls rise up from the river. "What was that?" someone asks. "I don't know," someone says. "I didn't hear anything." There is splashing. There is laughing. There is shushing. There is stillness as you listen and the girls listen. "Hey! Who's there?" a girl shouts, and then there is a wet scuffle. You say nothing. You are deciding what to do when you hear the distant whine of an engine. "Someone's coming," a girl says. "Get down," another girl says. They giggle. Nervously. The whine of an engine grows closer, multiplies. It is not one engine. It is many. You see headlights arch skyward and then tip over the top of the hill you have just hurtled down. Motorcycles. The girls squeal. You ditch your bike behind the Skylark and crash into the woods, counting on the roar of engines to mask your animal sounds. Hide behind a cement piling at the base of the bridge. You can see the girls in the river beneath you, at a distance of twenty feet. They are teenagers. They are naked. Their clothes glow—white t-shirts, jean shorts—on the rocks at the edge of the river. The girls cannot get to their clothes. They sink their pale bodies into the dark water. They watch the bridge above them. They have forgotten about the way your bike tires sang. The motorcycles hit the bridge and the whole thing shakes. The girls smile with relief when the motorcycles have passed over, but they stay crouched down, listening to the engines slow at the stop sign half a mile away. The motorcycles do more than slow. They come to a stop. They idle. The girls look at each other, worried. One by one, the motorcycles turn around. The bikers approach the bridge slowly, revving their engines, holding the machines in check. You don't dare glance back, although you want to count them. You see fear on the girls' faces. Fear. Not delicious fright. The motorcycles cross onto the bridge. Engines cut off. Your ears ring in the silence. The girls edge toward deeper water. A man on the bridge laughs and the girls freeze. One of them is crying. You don't know when she started crying. Her hair is slicked down and wet. She has been trying to stay under, but she has to breathe. "Giiiirls," a man calls, singsong. "We seeeee you." That cannot be true. You do not think it can be true. Even with the moon it is a dark night and the view from the bridge would be at a wrong angle. More men laugh. Is there anything you can do? "Don't hide," another man says. "We won't hurt you." More laughing.

And then, one man kicks his engine back to life. The others do. They turn their motorcycles around and roar off, as suddenly and as inexplicably as they have come. They do not slow for the stop sign. They scream through it. Heading east. "Oh my god," one girl cries. "What the hell? What the fucking hell?" another girl asks. "Go, go, go," a girl says. They scramble for the bank. They struggle for their clothes, t-shirts and jean shorts stretching and sticking over wet limbs. One girl cannot find her clothes. "Wait, hold on, wait," she keeps saying. "Come on," another girl says. They are scrambling up the bank. You could call out to them. You could say to the girls, Hey. It's okay. You're safe. The girl who is being left behind is the girl who was crying. Even if the other girls get up out of the river bottom you could say to her, It's okay. You're safe. The motorcycles are gone. It is just you, now, watching them. The girls are frightened, but they are safe. The girls are safe, aren't they?

About the Author

Laura Krughoff's debut novel, *My Brother's Name*, was a finalist for a 2014 Lambda Literary Foundation Award. Her current novel project, based on her Pushcart Prize winning short story, "Halley's Comet," follows the personal and political lives of two women as they navigate the decade between Massachusetts legalizing same-sex marriage and the U.S. Supreme Court overturning the Defense of Marriage Act. Her short fiction and essays have appeared in publications ranging from literary journals such as *The Threepenny Review* to the Gay Voices section of *The Huffington Post* to the podcast of the Chicago-based story-telling performance collective Second Story. She teaches in the English Department and in the Gender and Queer Studies Program at the University of Puget Sound.

www.ingramcontent.com/pod-product-compliance
Lightning Source LLC
Chambersburg PA
CBHW072035170626
46811CB00008B/3087